OTHER BOOKS BY VICTORIA REDEL

Where the Road Bottoms Out (short stories)

Already the World (poetry)

Loverboy

◇ ◇ ◇

A NOVEL BY

Victoria Redel

Winner of the S. Mariella Gable Prize

Graywolf Press

SAINT PAUL, MINNESOTA

Publication of this volume is made possible in part by a grant provided by the Minnesota State Arts Board through an appropriation by the Minnesota State Legislature, and by a grant from the National Endowment for the Arts. Significant support has also been provided by the Bush Foundation; Dayton's Project Imagine with support from Target Foundation; the McKnight Foundation; a grant made on behalf of the Stargazer Foundation; and other generous contributions from foundations, corporations, and individuals. To these organizations and individuals we offer our heartfelt thanks.

Graywolf Press also acknowledges the generous support of the College of Saint Benedict and the Teagle Foundation.

Published by Graywolf Press
2402 University Avenue, Suite 203
Saint Paul, Minnesota 55114
All rights reserved.

www.graywolfpress.org

Printed in Canada
Published in the United States of America

ISBN 1-55597-322-1

2   4   6   8   9   7   5   3   1
First Graywolf Printing, 2001

Library of Congress Catalog Number: 00-107649

Cover photograph: Ernest Haas, © Tony Stone

Cover design: Scott Sorenson

For Bill

Magic Boy

He stands on the chair draped in my red silk shirt, the sleeves knotted around his neck so that it falls, a shimmering cape behind him.

I am to sit—he has instructed me exactly how I must sit—hands folded, legs crossed at the ankles.

"Magically," he says. He lifts both his arms, a wooden spoon waves in the air.

"Like this," he says, his arms in a whiz, in a buzz of commotion.

I look at him. That sweet face. Serious, clever eyes. The ordinary light highlighted by touching his glorious rouged face. Has a mother ever loved a child more? But this is the wrong thing, smiling and looking at him with doting, motherly appreciation.

"Magically," he announces and he is all business and professional wizardry, "we are invisible."

I look with mock amazement at my hands, my arms.

"Oh, forget it," he flares flipping the red shirt cape and twirling so that his back is to me. "Magically, magically, magically," he intones. Here is the wooden spoon again, up like a commandment. "Magically," he exclaims, stern, certain, distant, "I am gone."

PART ONE

Loverboy

What Did I Call Him?

After he had been alive exactly nine months, I watched him in his twitching, clutchy infant sleep. "Now you have been theirs," I thought, his hand bunching around my finger, "for as long as you were safe inside and only mine."

Now I wake and think I hear him speaking to me, the musical insistence at the edge of his words.

"I am here," I try to say, but then I open my eyes and see people, too many people in this white room. And none of them is him.

Someone leans in over me, "She's trying to speak."

They parade in by twos and fours. Or, they enter alone, pause stiff-legged at the door. There is one with a blue tattoo spiraling up her freckled arm, an inked tail snaked under her white uniform. There is one who carries papers. One with a sterile cloth. Others I barely see, or see only pieces of them, bulky calves, a brown hand fumbling with a knob. I see a scar quarter mooned on a brown cheek. Clipboards. How much deprivation has been sustained? they wonder. They point. The hippocampus has been involved. They worry over my basal ganglia. They calculate my damage. Has there been paralysis, a visual fixation?

Many Clipboards scuff in and out of the room.

I am attached. Things drip and measure, machines pump, clean my blood, regulate air, trying to bring me all the way back to life.

"Expect seizures," says a White Coat going out the door.

In comes the doctor. In comes the nurse. In comes the lady with the alligator purse.

I hear him, somewhere, clapping and singing. I try to join his patty-cake.

"Hey! Quick! She's calling for the nurse," someone says.

But I am gone. Past the Clipboards. Swerve past the orderlies. Back to find wherever he is, lost on our trip, trying to find his way to me, his mother.

Yes, I named him Paul, but until he insisted, I never called him Paul.

I called him Pussycat and Sweetheart and Button and Sweetiepie and Sweetpea and Honeypie and Cutie and Babydoll and Sprinkle and Kiddo and Buck. I called him Cookie and Bear and Angel and Gooseboy and Ace and Spunk and Rabbit. I called him Pablo and Pablito. I called him Lovey and Love.

But most of the time I just called him Loverboy.

"Loverboy," I said when he was little, his mouth just a perfect tiny pucker, "You, Loverboy, are the loveliest thing on this earth."

What if he had not said it, not said that night without so much as a glance up at me from where he stacked his Legos, "Call me Paul." We might have just stayed there, inside our house with its milky, early evening light.

We might have locked the door and called it a holiday.

We might have snuggled on the couch just as Sybil and Marty taught me to do.

I gave everyone all the chances I could to give him back to me.

I would not have pressed on down the stairs into the garage.

Let me start with his teeth.

First there was the fretting agony of the first teeth coming in. Nights rubbing analgesics, an ice pack to press against his raw baby gums, a finger dipped in brandy, anything it took to stop the desperate bleating. Of course, there is always a mother who claims that for her baby it was uneventful. No spiking fever. No crankiness for her child, "Heavens," she wrinkles her nose, "no runny bowels."

But I was not that mother.

It was for my boy an agony.

Nothing is uneventful.

And then, just a few years later—hardly any time at all—the tooth falls out. And the child, look at him, ready for big teeth, he tries to speed it up. All that twisting, that horrible pressing, rocking, playing the tongue against the little chiclet, working the tip into the crevasses, feeling, perhaps, the point of the incoming tooth. Hours with fingers in the mouth. The constant wobbling of the tooth. As if a reward, a coin beneath the pillow, a measly token from a night fairy, could measure the agony of bone growing through bone.

But he could not remember that.

No, for my Pablito it was a delight, this promise of something grown-up, his permanent teeth.

It did not upset me. It broke my heart.

I am barely breathing now. I am almost there, far away, safe, with him. The IV, a vein of blind turns. My body rolls, a slow-motion spin toward the smash of light. I veer, my heart skids and the machine snaps on.

But what are they doing here? The aqua woman with messy kisses, none for the girl-child, all for the man, for this child's father who opens the front door each night and swings the mother, freshly showered, up in his arms, saying, "Sybil, I could not bear to be away from you another moment."

No other mothers now.

Not that non-mother, my mother, Sybil, and not these neighborhood mothers scolding, "No baby-sitter? Come on, don't you ever get a minute away from that child?" No fathers. Not even the one that, despite myself, I remember sometimes when I am holding my son, touching his sweep of black hair, the leafy night of forested places on his body.

No, only the child. My child.

It would do well to find a passion, Sybil said when she thought to dispense some motherly advice.

What I needed in the end was only to love the child.

Afternoons, when he was still little, I mounted him in a child's pack and with him riding high against my back, I walked. Out of our neighborhood, into the city where there were streets where shirts were hung on frayed lines between freight buildings. All the time I talked to him. *Laurel tree. Bench. Shop. Wheel. Brick.* I taught him the names of what we saw. Once, remarkably, on a narrow city block, we saw the carcass of a deer hanging by a rope from a window. More words. There was a word for everything. Even words invented for the pleasure of sound. We never got lost, we got *smoshkabibbled.* There were afternoons we *friddled.* As though we were the first, my darling and I, naming our very own world into being. We were gods then, together, those afternoons.

Later, when he could walk, he walked next to me. Hours walking, especially in rain, walking on puddled streets. "It is only water," I laughed. The few people we passed were hunched under umbrellas or had coats yanked pitifully over their turtled heads. For us there were never umbrellas. As if rain was something from which gods and heroes needed protection!

We waited under a railway trestle. A sudden water-fall cascaded over the sawed-off ends of the metal ties. We stepped out into the rain. While everyone else crowded under shop awnings, we skipped from one restaurant to the next, ordering a steaming bowl of noodle soup, a cup of warm almond milk. Then we cut holes in plastic bags and *frogaciously* jumped puddles all our way home.

Or we walked in a November mist, watched golden light brighten houses where we saw women in quilted mitts opening oven doors.

Mostly here, I hear women. Women talking, the cluck of their calibrated tongues. "Can she hear us?" "Look at this chart." The poke and probe of fingers and needles. Someone straps something against my chest. Next my arms are strapped.

"It's unbelievable, we're in another convulsion."

This motor of women and machines, they claim me.

"It's under control. I think we've got her stabilized now."

"Is she going to make it? Can she do it?"

Here is what I did.

I ate him when he was my powdery and juicy sweet boy who wanted to be eaten. He was my morsel. He was delicious in his rodeo pajamas and corduroy slip-pers squealing, "Tickle me more!" He bucked and kicked. I lassoed him close and tickled more. I rubbed his back as he fidgeted and thrashed his way to sleep. I wiped his nose. I put my pinkie into his tiny nostril when the mucus was hard, crusted into a tight pebble, and I worked to pick it out. I kneaded his stomach when he was crampy with gas. I cut out the knotted hair matted at the back of his head. I tilted his head to keep the shampoo from running into his eyes. I munched on his thick legs. I chewed on his buttocks. I kissed his lips. I let him suck the dried sticky jam off my finger. I put him—once he was so small!—on the changing pad. I cleaned an eye and, with a new cotton, the other eye and with more fresh cotton, the wrinkled skin under his neck and under his arms and, with a little alcohol, I cleaned around the stubby umbilical clamp. And when his penis was still crusty with blood from the doctor's cut, I used a Q-tip to dab salve to that. Then I lifted his feet the way you would lift a trussed chicken and wiped Chickieboy's lightly haired back and his bony behind. Or when he was sick, I held his head while he vomited into the metal mixing bowl or I caught his vomit in my hands when he could not get to the toilet on time. I wiped shit from him and put a little cream on the puckered anus skin when it was raw and red from whatever in his diarrhea made him itch and sting. I touched him all the time. His cheeks, the lids of his eyes, the palms of his hands. I should have touched him more.

"My eyes," he said, "you have not kissed my eyes."

Every part of him I kissed. My hair trailed above my kisses so that in the high heat of August when my hair was clipped off my damp neck, he would say, "No, I need your hair with the kisses." But when he said, "Kiss me there," pushing my head toward his perfect miniature cock, I stopped. I shook my head, my hair shaking in a tickley way on his chest and said, "No way, Loverboy, there will be no kisses like that."

There is no falling in love like the falling in love with a child.

What a thing it is, love! How love amazes us, at first turning us ever deeper into love. How it thrills, and thrilled, dizzy, descending, we imagine there is no end to the depth. And how, finally so deep in love, we panic. How did we get here? How long will it be until our circumstances exhaust our love? Or will our circumstances outlive the love?

Either way, how will we survive?

There is no falling in love like the falling in love with a child.

His breath, that sweet dazzle, the thousands of tiny exhalations. Or a night he is ill, his body a damp burning against my chest and I do not sleep listening to each wheezy thick breath as he sleeps sitting up in my arms.

Who has ever wanted to share a love? I had done everything to make this child. I refused to share.

I listened to the smiles that said, "He is ours now, lady."

I packed us up. It was as easy, as quick as leaving all the rental rooms I had ever left. A few boxes loaded into the backseat, that is all we would need. This time we would roam farther than the city or the island with its washed-out bridge. We needed to speed very far away. That is why Mrs. Yarkin came back all these years later, why she appeared, whispering to follow her. We would find a road not on any map. She would show me where she had driven off to in the middle of the night.

I was never going to be ready to give him up.

We Are Going

"Okay, Paul, it is time to go."

"Where?" he asked not even looking up from the red-and-yellow Lego school he had been building since his bath. His voice had an edge of annoyance that no longer surprised me.

Really, my actual presence, I suspect, had become a disruption.

"My secret," I said offhandedly, as if I really did not even care for him to know.

Finally he looked up. "What?" he asked. In his voice I heard the first genuine interest in anything I had said in weeks.

"What secret?" he asked. "You have a secret?" He was surprised, I could tell, at the very notion that I might have a secret.

I laughed. "How much would you like to know?"

"Whatever," he said turning back to the lopsided staircase he was building.

"Paul," I said, "Paul, we are going now."

"In a second," he snapped.

"Loverboy," I said quietly, "would you like to drive?"

Now, just like that, he was up and rubbing close to me, saying, "Really, Mom? I can drive! But I can't really drive, Mom, you know that, right?"

I almost began to correct him—*not can't, use cannot*—but I thought the better of it. I would sacrifice my dislike of contractions, that sloppy disrespect for the beauty of each word. Contractions—isn'ts and don'ts—these are telltale signs of people who scarcely care for what they say at all. I wanted to remind him that we must always be alert to what we say and how it is said. But now I had to keep going. I had his interest. He had come to me. He leaned close to me in his worn pajamas with their horsemen and horses. He felt so small again in those pajamas.

"It is a lesson," I said and thought that if he comes any closer, up into my lap, then we will not go. I will not take him into the fixed-up garage. We will not have to take this trip.

"A lesson? Like in school?" he stood back, suddenly suspect. "But you aren't even a teacher," he frowned, looking at me with all the challenge of these last months.

"Driving school," I said with authority and could not help myself, adding, "*are not.* Two words."

"But what's the trip?" he said with a mixture of interest and suspicion.

"The trip will come after the lesson. You will see," I said. "But first clean up your Legos."

It seems crazy that I bothered to ask him to clean up his little mess of Legos. But, despite myself, I have always needed a tidy house. This was one of the reasons I never wanted to live in a house, certain that I would be forever about the house, cleaning up, arranging, making things look right. I have seen other homes with their jumble, that lived-in chaos, newspapers and clothes everywhere, and especially the plastic toy clutter that overtakes the home. I was horrified and also a bit envious of the way they went about unfazed by the sprawl. But I envied them in the condescending way one envies an idiot.

"We will drive," I said, "when those Legos are all put back."

Our night had started as such a good night. He had let me in to bathe him and, of course, at first, I claimed it as a victory. It was a victory. After those nights of taped-up signs, rough-markered letters blocking, KEEP OUT! But that night it was, "Come in, come in. I want to show you how long I can hold my breath. Will you count?" Rinsing his hair, I delicately supported the back of his neck as he tipped his head under the running faucet. I did not let him get any soap into his eyes. He showed off his underwater breathing trick. "Count again," he said when he came up for air. Then he stepped from the bath into a towel I held out for him, and let me pat and rub him dry, his arms, his back, the terry cloth soft under my hands. I was in heaven. He even let me put him into his pajamas.

But after the bath he was, suddenly, all tooth business. Working the tooth. Working the tooth. It was a thready, horrid thing, bloody gums, and the tooth hanging by a thread.

"Just stop it now!" I shouted.

He barely looked at me. He barely noticed that I had shouted. He was so distracted by his determined working of the tooth. All that playing with it, I could not stand it. I hated his eagerness. I hated how each baby tooth, so lovely to me, seemed to insult him. I could hardly say, "Do not brush them," when he started with the blue toothbrush, though I wanted to forbid his brushing, his pushing at the loose tooth with the soft bristles. And, finally, I did say, "Stop it now. You will ruin your gums and make them bleed," when, of course his mouth was bloody already, him working the bristles under the tooth.

Then, when he understood that for now it was hopeless, he set to work building with Legos.

"May I build with you?" I asked.

"It's my school I'm building," he announced. He had turned against me. He had turned back to building a desk for that teacher, Miss Silken, with her penciled, smiley faces poisoning his class work.

He only wanted me if he could say, "Look, Mom!" with a triumphant bloody-gap smile. I would have to praise him, inspect the ridged hole where the tooth had been.

I would have to say, "I hardly recognize you."

No, I could not stand it. I would have to praise the loss. He was in such an unforgivable hurry.

And now he was building that school with its little blondie teacher, his slim-hipped, impossibly earnest Miss Silken. Silky Silken. And the others. The good-watchdog secretary, Mrs. Pomeroy and the ever helpful Principal—don't forget, children, that is principal, P-A-L.

"Loverboy," I said, "come on, let me help you build. We shall build together."

"Mom, you're not allowed in my school anymore. And I told you, call me Paul."

So then there were no more chances. It would not help to snap at him, "That does not look a thing like your school. And, say *it is*, not *it's*."

It was time to go downstairs to the garage and buckle us safely in. First he could have his driving lesson. Then it would be time to leave.

"Okay, Paul," I said. "It is time to go."

Lemons

I cannot say why she was there at all. Perhaps an invitation had been made on my part, some effort, I suppose to situate myself among other mothers because, briefly, early on, I mistakenly imagined that this was the correct thing to do.

"This is one easy baby," she called to me.

I was in the kitchen fixing iced concoctions. It seemed important to me then that I come walking out of the room with two terrific iced drinks in tall blue Mexican glasses. That it be a little fantastic, that I had everything entirely under control, that, despite the heat and the new baby, I had time to whip up great cooling drinks. His skin was blistered from the heat. I had left Loverboy in the room with the woman. I felt somehow that it was expected of me to leave him under her supervision. It seemed part of it all, to just leave my son in a room with a woman I hardly knew. It was as if motherhood had made all women suddenly people to be entirely trusted.

I hoped that she would not notice his rash.

I sliced the lemon in thin, thin sections.

I heard the woman singing. I did not really like hearing such music, if the song could be called music, in my house. It was one of those most unattractive songs that people sing in the presence of babies. I said nothing. She had not said anything about the horrible rash that rose in blotches across his face and neck. Even his fingers were thick with angry raised bumps. I forced a few dance steps as I slit the lemon slices so they fit over the lip of the Mexican glasses. Even if she had noticed his rash, I was forgiven.

Loverboy began crying. The mother called out, "Don't worry. I've got him. I've got it under control. He's fine."

She made cooey sounds. "That's a nicey nicey boy," she said and I imagined her bending close to him, maybe even touching the rash I could not make go away no matter how I bathed or powdered or dried him. I did not like her looking at him but I made myself stay in the kitchen. "Are you sure?" I asked and she was already answering, "God, it's not like I haven't spent the last year with my own crying baby."

He quieted.

"This is one easy boy," she said. I thought, she is better with my baby than I am. I wanted to get out to him. But I washed sprigs of fresh mint and placed them decoratively poking up out of the glasses.

The tray looked good, the wonderful cobalt blue glasses, the sharp lemon color, and the little frill of green leaf. I was pleased.

I carried the drinks into the room.

"That was quick," I said cheerfully. "You must teach me your tricks."

She was standing with her back to me, over by the window. She laughed, "No sweat. There are no tricks. You've just got an easy kid."

"Really, you think so?" I asked, suddenly feeling that she had some greater knowledge of my child, some evaluative sense of him that was beyond my rather limited experience.

"God, yes," she said. "He calms. He takes easily to people. What else could you want?"

I did not think I wanted an easy boy.

"I have your drink," I said, unsure of what exactly I wanted.

She turned. "Oh, I need it," she said with a open smile. Her blouse was unbuttoned and I saw Loverboy crooked up in her arms. Her large breast was mashed against his face and her wide brown nipple plugged in his lips.

She smiled. "Look at these splendid drinks! Drinks for everyone," she said, stroking Loverboy's cheek.

He was sucking, his cheeks working, and there was a wet, filmy sheen on his face so that his rash seemed brighter. I rushed for him. I dropped the drinks. But I had also dropped to the ground so that I was on all fours coming at them to get him off of her huge nipple, to get that squashing breast off his raw face, but I was also wiping up the mess, picking up splinters of blue glass, watching his eyes drift closed with the same pleasure I saw when he sucked at my breast. I was at her knees; my hands filled with lemon and broken glass.

"Oh, what are you doing! Please be careful," the woman shrieked, snugging my son tighter against her chest. "You'll get someone hurt if you don't watch out."

Paul

Now, Loverboy, I will call you Paul. From now on—you
win—it is as you wish, only Paul. Not My Baby or even
Paulie as I called you when you were three and loved
all things ending with the long E sound. Birdie. Cookie.
Puppy. Paulie, I said as you crawled over me and into
my bed, the morning light not yet sifted in through the
curtains. Your hair damp, your breath a tangy sweetness. "Paulie," I said, "it is not yet morning, Sleepyboy.
Back to sleepy." But now, no more names, no silly di-
minutives. I promise I will call you Paul.

If there are no slipups, then you will give me another chance.

Come for me, Paul. Come into the room past the
Clipboard Men and the whirring, beeping monitors, the
tubes that drip every kind of unkind, unimaginable life
into me. Come past the nurse with her silly dragon tattoo, her yin-yang tattoo, her plugged-in electric foun-
tain of life. Walk past the gawkers. Come for me, Paul.

The Buddha Boy

I could argue that my first mistake was that I taught my child to walk. This argument is contrary to what is said in most books on development. A child, in these books, develops of his own accord, each child coming upon and then through predictable milestones—rolling over, sitting up, scooching, creeping, crawling, the child first standing in his crib, then cruising through rooms holding chair legs, table legs. The sudden lurching first step. The wobble. The fall. The parents' delight. Days pass and the child will not repeat the step. The parents plead and coo. They despair of the child walking ever again. Then one morning, as if it is no big deal, as if walking were always part of the body's vocabulary, as if all the waiting were a deliberate action against the parents, here is the child, pitched headlong, running toward the road.

Not Paul.

He sat. I could have called him Buddha Boy. I was not unhappy. I was simply ready to get on with things.

"Come," I said. "Walk to me."

"Watch up," I said. I opened the door to the bathroom and ran the tub, dropping in two capfuls of the blue bubbles that he liked. In went his boat. In went his floating red ball. In went his mama, fully dressed.

"Come on," I said cheerfully.

He sat waving his delicious baby arms.

"Come on," I said, sitting down into the bubbles. I played with the boat. I ran his boat up my wet shirt. I rode it over my head. I submarined and torpedoed and mischiefed about with his toys.

"Uppy," whined this talking boy who would not walk. "I want uppy," he whined.

The boat sped up my throat and I caught it in a weedy thrash of my hair.

He whined and I played. More and more terrifically I played, making great splashes and bubbly creations.

Then he was up and walking to me. His arms out and his legs in a stubby-legged waddle.

I said not one word. I showed not a pip of surprise until he was at the rim of the tub. Then I smiled and said, "Oh yes, Young Prince. Please, Lord Waterboy, please step in."

Jasmine

There were nights they called to me, "We're in here." I hurried down, stood in the doorway, and recited facts for Marty and Sybil.

The Siberian Tiger needs to eat twenty pounds of meat a day to sustain itself in cold weather. Sliding Friction occurs when a solid body slides on a rough surface.

They looked up from the tangle of their embrace on the couch.

"We have some smartie," Marty said, drawing Sybil closer in his arms. She kissed him while she glanced at me.

"What are we going to do with her?" she laughed, tucking herself impossibly tighter under his arm. They continued cooing and touching, praising each other as one might praise the surprising growth of an exotic plant in the yard.

Occasionally I was brought along on jaunts to

nurseries in a sudden mania to have an English garden such as the gardens one might imagine Vita Sackville-West and Sir Harold Nicolson cultivated over the many years of their odd devoted life together. That we had only a narrow and shady yard mattered not a jot. But soon I could see that their passion for making a garden was forgotten and they walked the gravel nursery rows as if on a stroll in an arboretum. The plants were hardly compelling to them, the broad canopy of leaves was simply another elegant backdrop for a stroll.

They walked up and down the same paths, her bare arm laced with his, as if they had not noticed they were passing the same plants. They spoke, as they always did, in a whisper. Sybil paused before a rhododendron. She stroked the thick waxy petals.

"You want that one?" he asked, touching her hair. He was always ready to please her, ready to hoist it from its burlap-bundled roots. His life justified by her whims.

"No," she said, looking at Marty with a pouty smile. "I just wanted to touch," and she moved on to the infant lilacs.

"Is that something you want?" He was so eager, and the impatience in his voice was just his excitement to get back to the house to be alone with her in the privacy of their yard.

Finally she chose, settled on a perennial, three pots of indian jasmine, which needed more light than they had in the shaded yard. The tags said jasmine needed warm dry weather. It floundered in northern zones, must be taken indoors in winter. They shooed away the information.

Later in the yard Marty said, "Do you want it here? Or here?" and made a show of planting, digging with his shirt off, pulling rocks, lugging them about so that Sybil came up behind him to stroke his arm and cooed, "Darling, to see you like this, I insist we must make a whole garden."

But after a hearty dousing, they forgot the plants. Or maybe they did not quite forget so much as that they never made it back out to water the jasmine or cut back its growth. The plants did not come back or came back as thin, stubby plants with little promise of flowering. And, yet, somewhere in late summer, as they sat at the kitchen table with their rolls and tea, suddenly there was the drift of Indian Jasmine. Marty looked up. He hardly even remembered that out the window there was a yard. And, if he recalled a nursery it was as a charming park he had once visited with Sybil. For him there was only Sybil. He marveled, "Darling, I could eat you up with that new perfume."

With that same distracted look, they glanced up occasionally as I recited facts I had memorized. I was a trinket they had brought home. I hurried back to my room with its neat stacks of books, its shelves of labeled experiments and collections of mica. There was always something else I needed to read, another fact to be memorized. I never stuck around to hear if they asked me to go on and please tell them more.

In the Too Bright Room

The first time I took him to a crowded park after he could walk, he scooted off, out of grasp. Teenagers ranged in gangly romantic tackles on the lawns. He wriggled out of my hold and was off. Someone drifted in front of me blocking my sight. Then all I could see was a thicket of strollers, their wide, loose-limbed bodies blocking the path. For that moment I imagined everything that would happen. The edge of a pond. The gnawing park rats. A split in the path. Who were the men on benches hiding behind papers or boldly watching people? There were arms to get around, the glare of noon, a fat couple coming together in an embrace. I swatted and pushed.

It feels like that when I wake here, when I float up to the surface, it feels the same, just like that.

This too bright room.

There is a man in the corner. He sits with his book closed and watches me.

The rest come in and knock about me, fix a monitor that graphs the level of my life. Or the cleaner comes with his push broom and sharp ammonia fluids. The bed shakes. They drop pumps. Into everything they knock. They break more than they fix. And they always talk and talk, trying to gather between them a clump of facts—cardiac rate, cell count, lesion scan— as if they might then pull from that messy heap enough facts to string together a chain of what,where, and why.

Or under the overhead glare, they say nothing.

They change the drip, yank, are rough.

To have to touch me—it makes them uneasy.

People lean over me, near me, in front of me, blocking my way, where I need to get to, where he is, toddling, just out of reach, in the place we were going to together, and here I am, still stuck on the other side, with people, people, all strangers blocking me from getting over to my boy's side.

Spy Time

Or I could say that my mistake was that I had not thought of Lenny, the teenager who took care of my lawn.

I am wrong to say that Lenny took care of the lawn. He was, after all, only a teenage boy. I never expected much care to be involved in his job. Clearly, I am wrong to even call it a job, that title confers the status of clear hours of work, a set of agreed-upon expectations. There were always patches of lawn he forgot to cut, as if midway through he thought of what he must be missing at the beach, his thoughts rolling inevitably to a girl or a basketball. He might leave a pile of clippings or he might mow through a bed of flowers, lopping off glossy blooms. He never arrived on time even on those few days we agreed on a set time. Instead he simply showed up, pulling on the stuck metal of the dented garage door. We could not help but know when he had arrived, announcing himself by his noisy habits, dragging the mower and banging into more things than I thought there even were in the crowded garage. He was always there in a clatter, always knocking over a garbage can so that from wherever Loverboy and I sat quietly reading, one of us, laughing like at a punchline said, "Lenny's here."

No, Lenny was less a lawn service and more an entertainment, a sort of game for Loverboy and me.

I mean Paul.

Forgive me. That is what I meant to say. For Paul and me.

I tell Paul that we are spies. Outside, the teenage boy, Lenny, is mowing the front lawn.

"Crouch down, Killer," I say, kneeling by the window, "we are keeping surveillance."

Paul crawls onto my back. He leans over me ready to bang on the window. Softly I hold his hands away from the glass.

"We do not want the enemy to see us," I whisper.

Lenny has been out there for a while. First his T-shirt was rolled up so that it stuck high on his chest. Now he has pulled it off and stuffed it so that it hangs from a pocket of his jeans. He is at the age when suddenly a boy takes off his winter parka and, my God! he is not a boy anymore. He pulses to something on his earphones. He shakes his neck back and forth. His neck seems to have thickened overnight; it seems wider almost than his head. His back is startling, newly muscled and cut, a creature to be touched. The thing is, I can see that he knows it. No, not that I am watching, but that he is now one who is watched. He can already feel how this spring or summer a girl he has always known will slip her fingers under his shirt and he will be dizzy and wild and uncertain.

"Stop!" I shout as he rides the mower right over a bed of tulips. The heads, my glossy, gorgeous tulip heads, shred under the blades.

"What is it?" demands Loverboy, scooching higher up my back.

I watch Lenny twitch, looking back toward the house. He does not see us at our spy game. He darts about sweeping stems into a pile with his bare arms. He looks guilty and, what can I say? I enjoy all the quick, jerky guilty motions, the way he keeps scanning the yard as he pushes the broken-off flowers into his yard cloth.

I tell Paul that I am telling the criminal to stop. He has a turn, shouting stop so loudly I have to tell him that we are being chased by counterspies and we must be silent or our lives will be in danger. I hold Paul down close against me, scrunching us down so that we cannot be seen.

Then Lenny is up again, unfazed, dragging the mower behind him, his body yanking angrily to some song that twists in his ear.

Is That Your Boy?

Once, in another park, he actually got himself lost.

It was late afternoon. We had been out together roaming the streets. Roam Abouts, we named them. Roaming to find nothing, we found everything. A bank of bright roses deep in a woods, a man playing the lute on his front lawn. We walked past a playground where each time we passed I had arrogantly pointed to the mothers and children saying, "That is for the mothers and children who can imagine no better place to go."

Yes, I cultivated an arrogance. I thought us better than the others and I told Loverboy that we had imaginations that exceeded the confines of a regular playground. If we had walked past the playground a hundred times, then a hundred times I said to Loverboy that he must take a good look at what he saw when he walked past. We could go in, I said, if he wanted to, but would a god go to a playground already created and in decay or would he go to where there was no living thing and make a new world?

No doubt, the question is extreme. I wanted to cultivate the exceptional. To do so takes, I am certain, exceptional means.

This day, God knows why, just to test the waters probably, he chose the playground.

I did not flinch. I did not say, "Are you sure?"

We went in through the chain fence. And off bounded Loverboy into a tangle of children.

I stood over by the little slide, clearly unpopular compared to the high slide or the spiral slide. I watched him slip among them, easily caught and brought right into their games. It happened so quickly. He was their creature now, absolutely. I watched him hang upside down off of everything. He flitted from structure to structure, banging down seesaws, twisting chains until, letting go, he leaned and spun, stretched back, head back, shrieking and spinning and jumping off in a whirl, running to the next thing before the swing had even stopped its spinning.

I tried to see his body as a creature balanced, reaching beyond itself in some daring arc. He looked, instead, small and unexceptional. He looked like every other child. It was painful to see him look so ordinary.

"Which one's yours?" asked a mother who had positioned herself next to me.

I started to point. She said, "All I ask is that mine runs himself wild till he's ready to just drop asleep." Another mother came up and another so that soon I was in the middle of a line of mothers, like pickets in a yard fence.

I looked up to find him in the tumble and romp. All that could be seen was his red sweater in a thrash of limbs at the metal monkey bars. "That one is mine," I said pointing to a blur of kids.

"He's a darling," said a voice a few pickets down the mother-fence.

But he was off to something new, in a frenzy of play with the other children; there was hardly anything of my Loverboy left for me to watch.

I stood about with the other women. I remember not much of anything talked about. I believe we spoke of the weather. How good it was not to worry about the lost mittens and stuffing them into boots every time they wanted to run out. It was warm outside. I tilted my face up into the sunlight. I said one or two things to be part of the park conversation. I suppose I felt that if he could do it, I could do it. Perhaps even a resentful gesture—if he had gone off to the children, than I would go off to the mothers.

A mother said, "I thought I'd die if I had to stay in with them through one more day of rain."

"I almost killed them both last night," a mother said with a big smile. They laughed, the great conspiratorial laugh of mothers.

Then someone said, "Isn't that yours, over there?" and I heard the collective worried sucking in of breath as each mother scouted for her child.

There was a blur of children by the tall slide.

A nudge, a bump, someone saying, "Oh my, I think that's your boy over there."

I squinched and saw an ugly child. Bloody face, bloody shirt, a crying, wet, bloody boy, horrible with his face all twisted and red. He was dazed, weaving, a lost boy wandering on the playground. Then he came at me, the horrid child, putting his bloody face against my leg.

I flinched. It was as if a strange dog, a mongrel, a dog of uncertain quality had leapt on me. The boy was holding tight to my leg.

"Don't worry, I don't think it's anything serious," said a woman crouching close to the boy.

The other mothers handed me Kleenex and wet naps.

"I want to go home, Mama," he choked. "I want to go home."

And from somewhere, so far away, I thought I could hear my boy, Loverboy, calling my name.

I Was a Girl Who Knew Things

The longest consecutive chain of hydrocarbons is considered the parent. . . . Jawaharal Nehru was the first prime minister of independent India. . . . Maat, Min, Mut the Egyptian goddesses of truth, fertility and, lastly Mut, the vulture goddess or the mighty mother . . . . Evangelista Torricelli invented the barometer in 1644. . . .

I was known, as a child, as the girl who knew things. It occurred to me that this was a rather deplorable state of affairs regarding the abilities of my teachers and parents. What little I knew came from a book called nothing less than the *Book of Answers* and some novels I checked and rechecked from the library. I gleaned what I could from those novels—the back unpaved streets of London, a blue glass dish in a cupboard in Kiev, the raving Scottish King. Under the supreme neglect of Sybil and Marty who were preoccupied in messy attentions with each other, I sent myself out on Life Observations, which was simply my elaborate name for roaming through woods and yards to bring home samples of every kind of muck and fungus and stone for classification or dissection. It was, in fact, Marty and Sybil who presented me one birthday with the *Book of Answers*. I suppose it was an effort to absolve themselves of any and all remorseful pangs, a swift assurance that they were completing the parenting task. The book was a respectably thick single volume which, while handy, was ultimately a huge disappointment when I considered that this might be the sum of what there was to learn. However, I memorized as much of the book as I was able, which proved to be most of the book. When they were willing, I might distract my parents for a moment or two with the exact route of Lewis and Clark or make them smile when I said that the Bedouins each morning whisper their dreams into the ears of their sheep.

Yet the first time I looked into the red face of my infant, looking that first miraculous moment at his still-wet face, I understood I knew entirely too little. I could not recite for him all the elements on the periodic chart. I did not know how to tell the difference between the flight of a hawk and a turkey vulture.

I had fooled everyone. Marty and Sybil might be entertained. But there was no fooling my son. I wanted to whisper already into the unfurled little ear, one great poem by each of the world's greatest poets. But who were the great Sufi poets? Could I teach him for certain which mushrooms might be safely gathered and eaten?

Although I adored Emerson, I could not recite a single Emerson essay by heart.

Looking at him those first hours, as his face shifted, began taking shape, I thought together we would learn the rest of what I did not know.

Hide-and-Seek

I count one, two, up to twenty, listen to the scurry of him through our yard. But when I turn around the yard is silent and there is no sign of him. The trees are shed of leaves and, mostly, the lawn well raked.

"Ready or not here I come!" I shout and when there is no reply, no accidental flash of a coat sleeve, I feel a panic that I am alone. He has run off to hide in some other place.

"Ready or not," I repeat. How foolish this fretting. No doubt Paul is there, barely hidden behind some shrub.

"Here I come," I say trying to brighten my voice.

I want to find him in a great rush. "Got you!" I will say, scoop his lean body up in my arms, his legs kicking with caught delight. Instead I see all the narrow places in a yard a small child might wedge himself. I want to snatch him up, but know I must make a show of looking, that I must not find him when I find him, I must look right past where he has crouched behind the stripped rhododendron bush. "Hmm, where is my Pablo?" I must say. "Perhaps I will never find him." And I hear how he will laugh, his whole body shaking with pleasure at his own sneaky cleverness. I will raise the clowning pitch of my worry, "I shall be so all alone if I do not find my hiding son." I will lament. I will pretend not to even hear his muffled squeals.

I crouch through the yard, a pantomime of a sleuthing predator.

"Are you behind the tree?" I ask, circling a thin birch. I imagine he watches the silly slapstick of my looking. Around and around the tree I scout, pretending that I have missed him the first time.

"Would there be a boy hiding in the rhododendron?" I ask pushing open the matted branches, ready to see him.

But there is no hiding boy.

Again it occurs that he has wandered too far in search of a good hiding place. Soon I will be running through the connected neighborhood yards screaming, "Come out, come out, wherever you are!"

"I know where you are now!" I call out. I move in even more exaggerated movement through the yard, seeing myself only as the gesture of how he might see me from his hiding spot.

I peek for his feet under the hedge of shrubs that grow close to the house. I look in improbable places, as if when I open the screen door I expect that he has actually fit into the narrow place between the screen and front doors.

"You are some clever boy," I say loudly. "Hey, Fooling Boy, you have your mama completely bamboozled."

I say a mantra of our made-up words. We love the sound of words, the tinny knock of *clang*, and the sudden way our stomachs pull at the sound of *riptide*. We love the clean bite in *starch*.

And it seems to Paul and to me that great words lead us to greater words and to discoveries like all great explorers, like all the other great thinkers. Emerson made lists of words in his journal—dip of the balance, pot valiant, obverse, horseplay, yean, drill herald—claimed he felt the poorer for not having used these words. Victor Hugo went off to dinner parties insisting on speaking the briefly popular invented language of Solre-Sol.

For all intense and porpoises, we say.

We keep lists of words to try out. After reading our first book on weather, we were on the lookout for an opportunity to say *haboob*, or *flaschenblitz*, or *eye of the storm*. Lying on the grass, we hunted clouds on the lookout for a *mackerel sky* or *mares' tails*. Words were banished simply for overuse. We kept a list of words that seemed all wrong. The way they sounded was nothing like what they were meant to mean. If trick is a ruse, than why isn't trickle a particular antic? And pick and pickle? Was the pinkie pinker than the thumb? Abominable led us to abdominal, which raised for Paul the candy question. If cavities were a reason not to eat candy, why were we born, he argued, with a big one in our belly?

I seek but I am not finding him. When I see a leaf pile, with hardly enough leaves to cover him, my heart races. That sounds so foolish to say. But my heart races the way it might race to unexpectedly catch sight of someone you have thought about but not heard from for many years. Crossing the yard, I see how skimpy the trees look without leaves, like props, really, more than growing trees. I straddle the leaf pile. He must be there and when my hands reach into the wet mass of leafage, I keep stirring, pulling at the pressed layers as if it were a deeper pile than I know it is.

He has gone too far.

"Come out, come out wherever you are!" I call, panicked, angry.

I consider the house, him hiding behind the rack of coats. Or the garage with its cluttered shelves and piles of junk.

I look around embarrassed that he will pop up, saying, "You lose, Mama."

I shriek, "Loverboy, Loverboy, Loverboy," hardly waiting enough between shrieks to hear if he answers.

I have no idea how much time it takes me to register his tiny voice signaling: *beep beep beep beep beep beep.*

I close my eyes. I count to twenty, pretend to open my eyes to a brand-new game of hide-and-seek. He could be anywhere, even in a place where I have already looked.

Has the light shifted so that it seems as if I really might have opened my eyes into a different yard, a yard with more trees and thinner trees? I face the corner of our yard that edges a straggly woody strip separating our yard from the neighbors'. There is no flash of arm among the maple saplings.

But then, just before the trees, there is our excavation mound.

We call it the mound, though it is hardly a raised piece of ground, where after one hard rain, Paul and I had seen a smooth lip of glass. We said this belonged to our ancestors and began a formal excavation. Carefully, we unearthed the blue handle of a ceramic cup, colorfully painted pieces of broken plates. For weeks we dig and sift, record the finds of our rope-griddled site. We are archaeologists trying to understand the story of our ancients. In spring when the crocuses poke forth, we honor the planter of the bulbs. "How long ago?" asks Paul, trying to glue together a complete plate. It is all in the time before us, I explain to him, when others roamed this yard. And who were these people who left dishes outside in a far corner of the yard? We each propose a theory. A child, Paul suggests, out all by himself for a special picnic. Caught in an unexpected downpour, he leaves all his plates and cups out in the rain. I say it was a woman. She came out in the dark after everyone else had settled in their beds. And, as if she can pacify The God-of-Safe-and-Happy-Homes, each night she breaks a piece of what she loves best.

I walk over, shake off the panic, even anger, that mixes in me.

He is lying flat in the shallow excavation, his eyes

closed and his arms crossed over his chest in an effort to squeeze into the small trench.

"I found you," I whisper.

I lean over and kiss his perfect closed lips. Not right away does he open his eyes or begin to smile his triumphant smile. I watch his face. He is everyone who has ever slept in every fairy tale with a bit of apple stuck in a narrow throat passage, a potion given by a jealous rival. He is that mortal coveted by every god. And in the long second that I wait, in the terrible second before he springs awake with a "fooled you, Mama!" I think I am waiting for the ancients to decide whether I have sufficiently honored them. If the right dish has been broken and offered. And if this time I will get my son back.

What Happened Just Behind Them

Other afternoons we went down to the city to catch a show or simply to walk so that as Sybil said, blotting lipstick into a tissue, she could watch other women wither with envy as she strolled with such a smart-looking husband.

I trailed behind.

She held onto Marty but not as I saw some women who clutched and pressed against their men. But neither did she seem to flutter, her arm a papery thinness against his linen suit. Even from behind them I could see she had weight. Although she was thin in her aqua sleeveless dress, there was some substance to her hold. She walked half turned to him, as if he were less the man beside her than the one she was approaching, walking toward. And he leaned in so that their heads practically touched. They were caught up in their conversation. Then together I watched them turn to check to make sure I was still behind them, somewhere in sight.

They smiled, even sometimes said, "Hey slowpoke, join the party." Then they turned back and Marty whispered something. Sybil laughed and swung her hair across his tilted face.

I checked in my pocket where I had wadded Sybil's used tissue. *My mother's lips.* I said it again, taking my time over the word *mother.* Then I continued the show I had begun blocks before. I jerked the muscles in my face, set a twitch in my neck that ran down to where my fingers cricked into a palsied freeze. I had perfected my fraud.

In front of me, Marty's tongue was a breeze against Sybil's ear.

I was, with each difficult step, a showstopper.

No one bothered to look at the good-looking couple ahead of me, that stunning woman in her aqua dress and the doting man, glued to her side.

I was the event.

I had perfected my theater. I was an elaborate street show that brought grief and disgust and fascination across the faces. I made them wither as I dragged my body forward like a neon flash—*help me, help me*—announcing the brilliant, spastic walk.

Bird

"Spy time," he shouts, running in to find me on the floor of the bathroom organizing the medicine cabinet. The cabinet, no matter how frequently I neaten it, is a clutter of tubes, bottles falling out onto the bathroom floor. I hate the constant disarray of it. And the look of all the medicines I find distasteful, especially the medicines for children with their hyperbolic labels. Cherry candy. Great grape.

"Come on! He's here!" Paul pulls at me. Then I hear the lawn mower jostled against the metal door, a garbage top clanging. It is not Lenny's day to mow the yard. But, when has that fazed Lenny?

"Yes, I suppose it is time to spy," I say, setting the bottles with droppers in a line. Paul pulls me to the window just in time to see Lenny idle the lawn mower while pulling his shirt over his head with the jerky quickness of a boy who has not yet learned about taking his clothes off.

"I want to do that," my boy says and he is vroom-vrooming an invisible lawn mower in circles down the hall.

I watch the T-shirt slip out of where Lenny has tucked it into his jeans and he tosses it onto the rhododendron bush, knocking huge pink petals onto the lawn.

"Soon I will be out there working," Paul announces, "and you will stay inside and spy on me."

I wander back to throw out the last of the medicine bottles with their obligatory expiration dates but soon Paul comes in saying, "Come quick! The spy, Mama, the spy! He is coming to the front door, Mama, and he has a bomb in his hands!"

But the bomb is a baby bird cupped in Lenny's galumphing teenager hands and Lenny, trembly, is saying, "I don't know where it came from. I swear I just found this on the lawn."

He holds it out for me to take. I am not afraid of animals, but I have never liked to touch the wounded ones, their shaky bodies, the fast pulsing fidget of their limbs. But what can I do? My son is watching. Push it back at him? Say, "Lenny, leave it out there," and point toward a pile of leaf cuttings?

I suppose I open my hands, but what it feels like is that Lenny is stuffing the bird at me, pushing it into my unwilling hands. Its little chest pumps in my palms. Part of what I do not like is the strange half-born look of baby birds, the frizzled tufted hair, those bulgy eyes, the beak that is too soft and seems not quite a beak.

It takes all my effort not to drop it.

That is what I want, to just shrug the bird away from me, to let it drop and be done with it on the front step. I do not find it difficult to understand how mother cats and birds discard or eat their young. The mother has taken every effort to hide her kittens, to keep them snugly out of sight in the back of the pantry closet. Yet here are those quick human hands, reaching to ferret one out, to hold the warm furry pulse. And now the kitten smells wrong, has the terrible stain of another animal upon it. And the other hungry kittens smell just right. Or the bird drops from the nest. The mother is so tired. She cannot even look over the edge of her twigs. It is gone, thinks the mother bird, it has left me.

"Where is the mommy bird?" He comes close to me, pulling at my arms so that I must lower my hands to his view. My boy is worried. He wants to see the bird. I can see it pleases him the way I cradle the bird. I can see he believes that Lenny the spy has brought the bird to someone who will take care of everything.

I hear myself say with the confidence of mothers in uncertain situations, "Oh, the mother bird had to go off for just a little while, maybe to the market. We will take care of her baby." Then I am all industry and instruction, sending Paul off for a cardboard jewelry box, cleaning out a medicine dropper, and showing Lenny and Paul how this little creature takes the sugar-water drops. I am the mother, and the boys, even big Lenny, are eager to see how I can take care of everything. I am all magically mother conjuring splints for the bird's broken leg with a hair pin.

I declare the bird will not die.

Lenny looks relieved when I tell the story about how the mother bird is off finding worms for the babies and she will be back with nutrients so very soon.

But Loverboy—what can I say?—he is smarter than Lenny, says, "How will she find her baby? We need to take it back out near the tree."

We walk in a parade out to the tree. Lenny says seriously, "Right here, I found the bird here," and he points to the grass below the tree. I set the jewelry box down. Loverboy holds my hand.

"Your baby is here," I call up to the nest I cannot see. "Do not worry, we found your little baby. And we have set his leg right and given him something sweet to eat."

"What if I'd run him over?" Lenny says looking down at the jewelry box.

"It is okay, Lenny, really."

"No, what if I'd really killed the bird?" he insists as if there is an answer and I must have the answer. Looking over at Lenny, his shirt still shoved down into the waistband of his jeans, I can see that suddenly the yard has become a dangerous place for him, full, I think, of all the things he might hurt, or even worse, I think, the things he might hurt and be forced by shame to care for. Now Lenny sees that the lawn mower, with its easy whir and quick shave of flower heads, is a weapon. But looking down at the half-dead bird, he is mostly afraid of himself, the way he has so carelessly swept petals into the yard cloth, secretly dumping the whole kit and caboodle into the trash can and zipping off on his bike to meet friends at the beach.

"We should all go now," I say. "We need to leave the little bird here or the mother will not come back for the baby bird."

You plan in your head the right answers, but the difficult situation, when it springs up, never quite fits the answers you have prepared. Perhaps you are honest. You tell him that everything that lives must die. When the bird dies—because, of course, the little bird dies— you and the child will dig a hole beneath the tree. You place the bird with its too soft beak in the hole. You teach the child to say something special and serious as you both scoop back the dirt. The child decorates with little stones the mound. The child cries a little and you hold him saying, "It is okay."

But that is not what I do.

I wait through the ten forays Loverboy makes to check on our baby bird. He comes inside each time more and more frantic. It is night and the mother bird has not come home from the market. The baby rests on the tissue bed we have made for it in the jewelry box.

Even after we have read our last bedtime story, he is still worrying, "Mama, what if a cat eats our baby bird? What if someone steals the bird?"

I rub his back, my hands feeling the delicate wings of his shoulder blades.

He squirms up, "I want to just make sure nobody

ate the bird." I settle him down but he is back up, "If I cannot go, Mama, will you go check? I will wait in bed. I promise."

It is dark outside and the big tree casts darker shadows across the lawn. At first I think the baby is not there and, for a moment, I believe she has really come for it. But my finger touches a wing. I feel squeamish and want to go back inside. I reach in and take the baby bird out. Its pulse seems slower or maybe its pulse seems quicker, I am not sure. But I am sure that if I do not take care of things the baby will be dead or more than mostly dead come morning when Paul wakes and quickly runs out to check.

A tiny neck should be easy to snap. And probably it would be if I were not so restrained and delicate in my twisting. I set its body back in the box and fumble under bushes to find a rock. I pick one up that is uncomfortably big to hold in one hand. I place the bird on the lawn and smash its tiny head with the rock. I am glad not to have to touch this crushed bird again with my bare hands, but then I realize I need to pick it up and toss it in a garbage bag.

But I do what must be done so that in the morning he will wake me, holding the empty jewelry box, saying, "She came. You were right. The mother came and got her baby."

It would be easier if Paul had been asleep when I got back, but he is sitting up in his bed waiting in the glow of the night light.

He looks so sweet in his little pajamas.

I hand him the empty jewelry box. "Look, Loverboy, the mama bird came for her baby."

"She got him?" he says amazed it has all worked out.

I pull him to me and say, "Of course, Kiddo, what Mama in her right mind would let her baby fall out into the world and not come quick as she could to bring him back home?"

"Will you stay until I fall asleep?" he asks, pulling the covers close around his face.

I sit on his bed and tell him the story of Prince Loverboy and the Magic Bird, and by the time the small bird takes him up on her back and they go to visit the moon, my Loverboy has settled into his sleep. But I keep on, keep telling him the story, hoping I can conjure a route to make my way into the place of his dreams.

Falling Icarus

"She's getting better?" squeaks a nurse and, once in the night, changing a drip, her fingers paw across my face. Sometimes I try to watch the Man Who Sits in the Corner All Day. He has a book but I never see him read. What if he is Jacob, come again to rescue me from a hospital? I want to ask him to *come out Little Jack Horner*, let me know just which one of the men you are. I try to say this but the tubes in my throat suck out a raspy, airless sound.

Out of the crank and whir of machines, I hear them like a challenge. "She'll make it," they dare.

They check their clipboards. Someone says the white-cell count is still too high. There are complications, a respiratory chamber, treatments.

"I'm not happy with her sed rate," a White Coat says.

"She's slipping again."

I showed Paul pictures. Falling Icarus. Daedalus'

unheard warning. Brueghel's boy dropping from the sky. I read him Auden's "Musée des Beaux Arts." No one would look up or even notice him.

I showed him Michelangelo's *Pietà*. "This," I told him, "Sweetiepie, is the saddest of all."

In the City X

I have noticed that most people have a specific city or town where they would like to live, marking periods in their lives by saying, "This is when I lived in San Francisco," or, "Surely I was happiest the year I lived in Texas." They yearn to be back on the coast of Maine. They rearrange jobs to settle in the suburbs outside Chicago.

This interests me not at all.

Only that I not live anywhere too long. Every city for me could be the City X. I live in the City of X, in the Town of X. It is temporary. My housing rental. Even later, with Paul, when I owned our house, it was simply a town where we happened to live.

This was true for that childhood with Marty and Sybil.

They looked up from their sofa, a worn blue love seat. "What a child," Sybil said, always surprised that there was still a child in their home. A child was simply another project they had undertaken together, like learning to sail, or a class in ceramics signed up for one winter. But the boat took up too much of the spring. It needed so much—scraping, painting, getting it out of dry dock—just to have it ready for the summer season. The lopsided clay pots took so many steps before they could be called finished.

No doubt about it, the White Coats and Clipboards would have, if they knew, extra notes, data for their charts, perhaps even a couple of Grand Rounds. Parents who never answered to mother or father. A seminar room's worth of raised eyebrows. Not that I shun the psychological, it has provided some decent writing of genuine interest. But it obfuscates Sybil and Marty's gift. From them I was given the chance to watch True Love. Its utter exclusivity. Boats, gardens, housecleaning, a child—mere diversions. All take away from the center.

No, there was no surprise that there was not a phone call from Sybil telling me Marty had only a few months left. I did not fit by that bedside. There was only a place for Sybil. I felt myself as a most distant relation.

And the final letter they wrote for me was an opportunity for them to see a hobby through to completion. I see Sybil as she lay down next to Marty. She held the pad and together they composed the short letter, stopping at length to recall their days together.

"At that graduation," Marty whispered, the cancer

having taken his voice, "darling, you wore the lavender suit."

It would do well to find a passion. They ended the letter with this familiar advice. When I tromped in from the woods with a bag of rocks for classification, they murmured to each other, "Geology might be a most absorbing passion."

When the lawyer sent the letter informing me that they had left a remarkable sum for me, it was not a real surprise. I was all the classes Marty and Sybil were grateful they did not take. I was all the projects that neither demanded devotion nor more than a trifle of their attention.

Harvest

He is four and singing from the *1812* Overture, la la laing the *Marseillaise.* He has been doing everything—bathing, eating bowls of cereal—with the Overture as his background music. In a chair or in the library letting Paul turn pages, plates of Da Vinci's drawings, Degas' studies. Where to start? Shakespeare, Bach's Mass in B Minor or his Concerto for Two Violins in D Minor. I need him to hear Child's Collected Ballads, and then again in Alan Lomax's *Folk Songs of the United States,* we listen for those same haunted melodies.

Everything was something. An amazing shared hunger.

All those other years of knowing and I had never really enjoyed it.

But with him—*Honey, come quickly, you must be here to hear the ecstatic build in Stravinsky's* Sacre du Printemps—it seemed I had found a feast, such a feast that was to be tasted with our fingers, and everything to be pulled apart, slowly, the delicious wings of rare cooked birds, juicy pockets of thinking to savor, that was the world for us, our learning, a sweetness, such harvest.

Mrs. Yarkin

When I left—stormed righteously past Miss Silken and
the Principal—it was Mrs. Yarkin who held open the
school door.

After all these years, a lifetime, and, somehow, I was
not surprised to see her. That she should appear to me
just then seemed perfectly wonderful. Perfectly correct, I suppose, is the best way to put it. I paused at the
door to smile at her. All these years I had been waiting
for her to come back and tell me where she had gone off
to with her sons. I was giddy. I had waited for her to
come back and take me away with them.

Mrs. Yarkin walked her delicate identical boys every
morning to my old bus stop. She was the only mother
who brought her children to the bus stop every day.
The boys flitted about her, skittering in front and behind her, a light froth of children. Her robe was silk, a

dark oriental blue, sashed at the waist. Her legs stepped through the robe as she walked.

Finally they arrived at the bus stop, one boy on each side of her, holding her white hands. I remember the rivery sound of silk as she knelt. Even the sound of her was like no other mother. She kissed each boy, a little kiss on their lips, and said, "Have the best day." Sybil blew me a kiss at the door with lips that, even from a distance, smelled of her breakfast. Each morning, there was one kiss for each boy. Then in the same liquid motion Mrs. Yarkin was up, walking back to her house. I watched her walk back. Like a gorgeous blue wave on the road. All of the bus-stop frenzy, the pushing and shoving, the singsong na na na's halted until she had walked the boys and kissed the boys and disappeared back into her house. We watched her as though she were the only real mother in the world.

Without her there, her sons looked off balanced, stilted, ill at ease. Everyday they were dressed in the same uniform. In spring, blue shorts and a white shirt. In winter, blue long pants and a pressed white shirt. Afternoons, coming off the bus, they folded into her arms like they had waited all day just to get back to her. Watching them walk home, which one of us children didn't mostly wish she were our mother.

Damaged permanently, those were the words I heard Sybil whisper to Marty.

One of those Yarkin boys had drunk something. Unsealed, unmarked, "a poison," Sybil whispered, "that had no business being under a sink." Sybil had heard it had been a dare, a boyish prank. She had been practically right there, Mrs. Yarkin, making, Sybil whispered, one of her overly elaborate dinners.

Sybil curled close to Marty. "You would think she might have taught those boys how to take care of themselves."

I tried to imagine what *damaged permanently* looked like. But all I saw was both boys perfect in their uniforms. I heard Mrs. Yarkin cheering, "Have the best day."

Sybil went with the other neighborhood mothers and stepped over the yellow tape that went around the Yarkins' house. Sybil wore her aqua dress and lipstick. It made sense to me that she dressed up to visit Mrs. Yarkin as she dressed to go out with Marty.

She touched the yellow tape.

That night Sybil and Marty came into my room and sat on my bed. They looked strange, out of place in my room. Sybil was still in her good clothes. Her lipstick had worn off, but there was a darkness to her lips that made her look more important than she usually looked. She said that all the parents in the neighborhood were talking to their kids. I thought about the whole neighborhood, about all the mothers with dark stained lips sitting on children's beds.

Sybil asked if I could be trusted not to do anything foolish. Marty asked if I knew not to taste any of the muck I collected out in the woods.

"Yes," I said, hoping they might stay with more questions.

"I told you," she said as she leaned in and kissed Marty on the cheek. I had the feeling I was not supposed to be listening. "This child could travel around the world by herself and we would have nothing to worry about."

I had no real reason to come to their end of the block. But I began taking an elaborate way home from the bus stop past the Yarkins' house. Each day they were outside, sitting in lawn chairs, one twin dressed in his white shirt and blue pants uniform. Mrs. Yarkin kept a rag in her hand.

One afternoon when I walked past, Mrs. Yarkin dragged her boy's arm up, shaking it in a slow, sloppy wave.

She motioned me up the front walk.

The boy's head was flipped forward. His eyes kind of peeked out from under his forehead. He rolled his eyes to the left and to the right until I felt them fix on my face.

"See, I told you," Mrs. Yarkin said, leaning in and dabbing at his chin.

She asked questions. Did I like my teacher? What instrument was I playing in the band? Did I have any talent for it? I tried, accordingly, to make myself sound serious and special, though I could not, for all my trying, imagine what might interest Mrs. Yarkin.

The boy made grottled, convulsive sounds. "Go on. Please," she said, if I stopped when he began his choking.

"Please," she said, folding her rag to dab at his chin, which was, I could see close-up, red and rashed raw. I tried to look right at him. But it was Mrs. Yarkin I saw smile when I said kids had stuck a sign on the cafeteria monitor's back saying, "Scream at me. I'm deaf."

The other twin walked into and out of the house. He looked as if he had nowhere good to go.

"Just go away," he hissed, passing close to me on his way to the edge of their yard.

"Just you go away," said Mrs. Yarkin with a flick of her hand and the twin boy walked back in the house.

"What were you saying?" she asked with excitement. "You were joking, right? A shop teacher with a wooden leg." She laughed and I started laughing, thinking how when I was in the Yarkins' yard everything I said actually seemed special.

"That's too much, isn't it, honey?" she said, folding and dabbing. "That's too good to be true."

It was true, I said. Everyone in school knew it was true. She could ask her other son, I said picking about in the weedy flowering grass. I sifted clover. I looked every afternoon for a clover with the fourth leaf to give Mrs. Yarkin for a lucky wish.

Then Mrs. Yarkin said, "Well, we're a little tired. Say your good-byes to your boyfriend."

I scooted myself over on the grass until I was close, under him almost, looking up into the hanging weight of his flopped-down head. I pushed myself up onto the balls of my feet. My lips felt the filmy wet of his slack lips.

"Say good-bye, honey," and as she had done before, she picked up his arm, shaking it until he gave me a floppy wave.

I waited until I was down the street to wipe my lips.

The next afternoon, after I kissed her boy, Mrs. Yarkin kissed me. Her eyes were open. The kiss was slow, a slow, open kiss that I was not certain would end. From then on, at the end of each visit when she kissed me, I struggled to keep my eyes open. But each day, against my efforts, I felt them flutter closed.

Then there was no one sitting on the lawn. The next day and then the next day too. I rang the doorbell. I imagined her securing the boy, belting him into his eating chair. "I'll be back," she said, hurrying down the three steps to the front door. I listed all the difficult things she must do before coming to open the door for me. I considered that her son was sick or that the other twin now had been damaged, too. But I was certain she would come to the door. She needed me.

I rang the bell again. She could not have gone anywhere. For certain she would have told me they were going. I was part of making Mrs. Yarkin's boy well. Had she not called me girlfriend? I had kissed him. She had kissed me. Waiting at her front door, I tried to think about where she had taken the boys.

I rang the bell for at least an hour.

I sat down and closed my eyes and tried to imagine a place they might have gone. I tried to imagine a place so remarkable that she might pass unnoticed. Buildings with women dressed exotically, threaded in gold and jewels and bells, streets alive with the sounds I had read about. India. Egypt. Markets where she might sit with her one son while the twin would rustle the streets bargaining with vendors, carrying back to her his satchel stuffed with ropes of sweet meat and drinks that made them sleep in the high afternoon sun. I saw lines of children all drooling and damaged and a great wailing of women.

I looked for a sign. Something she had left to point the way for me to follow. But all I could see was the road to the bus stop and back to Sybil and Marty's cluttered house.

The Magic Box

"Lenny," he repeats as if the kid's name itself is a kind of incrimination.

All the time, while this Dark Suit asks questions, I am working to remember how Paul sounded when he awoke tangled in a bad dream. I am working to remember the markings on his skin, a faint scar on his cheek from a jacket zipper.

He stands close to my cranked-up bed. Can I tell him about my relations with the teenager? He is a Dark Suit holding a pen. He quizzes me on the minutiae of each day. All random questions. Did I always use seat belts? What were my relations to Lenny? We played games, spying on Lenny while he barely took care of our lawn. Lenny was a noisy metal scrape Paul and I heard as the garage door yanked open.

And always, if I open my eyes, there is someone with a question. Nurses, men in robes and gowns and suits, more Clipboards and needles. The Tube Lady.

The Drain Orderly. All of them lean in listening for a gurgle, a moan, a clear group of words. Blood counts. Sporadic dysarthria and dysphagia, they announce.

"She's seizing again," they say, reaching for the chart.

"No, she's saying something," they say, reaching for pens.

If I could whisper up through the network of plastic tubing, I would say, "You want a confession?"

"Here is my confession," I would say, gathering the Investigators and Dark Suits, the Clipboards and nurses, the Concerned Ladies with their horrified frozen faces. "I was wrong. When he wanted smooches and kisses on every inch of his body, I should have excluded nothing. I should have eaten him up alive."

Instead, I say nothing. I close my eyes and look for Paul. I am opening all the shoe-box museums we have ever made, thinking there is a box, another box among all of the shoe-box museums and if I find it, I will find my old Loverboy.

Step into the box.

Shut the lid.

And magically we will be gone.

PART TWO

The City of Fathers

You Must Not Listen Now

You must not listen now, Paul. You who hear absolutely everything—from three rooms away you hear me thinking to myself. But now there is a part of this story, our story, that you must not listen to.

You and me, just us together. That is our story.

It is not yours to listen to the story of the fathers. Although one day—I was not at all prepared—you came home from that school of yours and asked me who was your father. There was no telling you there was no father because you had been to school and had been taught about the family. There were rules, facts—did I not know?—every child has a mother and a father. If I was so stupid to not know this, you could teach me what every first grader already knew.

Was he dead? Was he in another country?

Paul, you wanted answers.

You asked and asked until I had to answer. A cloud. A breath. The rain. He was like our wanderer Odysseus,

◇ 83 ◇

trapped and sleepy on an island, struggling still to come home. Some lusty god who found me by a weedy river.

"No!" you shouted, "no," and with each defiant "No!" I could see you pare away a little bit of our love and give it to this invisible father.

Every answer I gave was a fairy tale.

"No," you said, "no." There were rules in your precious schoolbooks.

Every answer I gave was wrong.

The Equation

.

Should I have told you, Paul, that there were two answers?

And that the first answer had the pristine beauty of an equation.

Many men equals no father.

I have waited for you on the unclean floors of strange bathrooms with my legs lifted, thrown back in the air. I have kept my legs raised for twenty minutes while semen traveled—passing through blocks and canals, the waving strands of cilia—in their upward search. On the other side of a shut door, a man, perhaps this one is the architect selected for the intelligent set of his brown eyes, dozes satisfied on a bed.

I have left the rooms of a Tom and a Peter, a Hans and a Flavio, men with names I could not even pronounce and men whose names I never learned. Architect, painter, roofer, botanist. They were my ready, sharpened tools. Careful to choose only men whose genetic flowering showed something splendid, I still had rather sufficient choice and each embodied a perfection—a gymnast's muscular back, a pianist's great reaching hands, a logician's classifying mind, a tongue that rolled through the dark hills of Catalonia.

They were the first fathers.

Walking through streets, museums, restaurants, libraries, I was like the great jewelers of the Byzantine sorting through full sacks of stones, saying, "No, not this one, too dull, without texture. I need to choose from more," and culling only a small collection of the extraordinary, the luminous, the ultimate.

That was how it was for me selecting the fathers.

I was the shrewd jeweler with the sharp eye and I was the rattlesnake who stores seven years of her mating to produce offspring. My body with its honed cycle of preparation and expulsion of the ovum. The ovum, that largest cell in the body, its hazardous journey toward the waiting nest of blood.

At first it surprised me that once the selection was made, the pickup was always swift. I had no clever technique. It was that simple. There was no need to primp or stain my lips to draw men to me. I stunned them. I was made stunning by my desire for you.

I was ready for you, my Ultimacy, as I had been ready for no one man. Ready for your cells to multiply. Ready to make the crown of your being.

I accepted the help I required. First the men, each gift from their bodies received with my silent benediction. And then there was substantial help from Marty and Sybil's legacy, money invested to give me all the cushion needed to make me free.

However, I have jumped ahead. Initially, I contacted a company, a donor bank. They sent lists, pages of pure information. The clean facts. Height and eye color. Medical history. Fair Danish skin. Blue-eyed Israeli, black-eyed Portuguese. It seemed clean. So purely mine. I could stay in my own room. I sifted through the facts. Selected donor 126. A check was sent to the donor bank and then I waited.

Never had the rental room seemed lovelier than in the days waiting for my delivery. There, in my tower of books, was the castle far from all the Victorian ethicists. My sparse room was a sumptuous boudoir those days where I lay about wondering how they would deliver the frozen seed.

But when it arrived, I grew uneasy. What arrived was a large corrugated box from which I pulled a heavy metal canister filled with dry ice. From a center shaft hung the five vials of number 126's donated semen. I felt squeamish. What exactly was I getting? How could I be certain? What if they had mixed things up, so that the small vials that I pulled from dry ice were not the donor sperm I had selected?

Alone in my stripped room, I went through with the five inseminations. There was no disappointment, given my dubious purchase, when conception did not occur. Rather, it was a relief.

The next month I sent away for nothing.

What I wanted was only you, the ropey muscles

from this runner, the precise hands of the violinist, the builder's vision, the historian's crooked smile, all the men that I brought into me to make this child that I would cherish.

I determined to be swift, discriminating, and reckless.

I am not being entirely coy or contemptuous but it was easy to secure the contributions. Decidedly none of these men would have been a man with whom I might have carried on a sustained union.

What is natural is only the bond between a mother and a child. I was not a brooder, sitting on a nest needing a helpful husband to bring anything home.

I never wanted a house and I never wanted a husband.

He said, "I'll see you again, right? What about Saturday? There's a performance of Mozart's *Requiem*." He spoke though the shut bathroom door. I was on his tile floor, my legs lifted and crossed in the air, the floor tiles sticky against my back, and I closed my eyes so that I could avoid the cluttered shelves, the mold-spotted ceiling. Clearly he had not been chosen for his cleanliness or his organization. I spotted him during intermission at the symphony. He was a dancer the way he glided through the crowd.

I checked my watch. Ten more minutes.

With a tentative knock on the door, the dancer said, "Are you still in there or what?"

"Sure," I said hoping it might pass for an answer to anything asked. Eight minutes. My hands slid deeper under my elevated buttocks, propping up the tilted pelvis.

This was his chance to join in as father. I was not the first woman to do this, I reminded myself. The traditional South American lowland societies functioned with partible paternity. Aside from the tribe's belief that more than one possible biological father might ensure a child's survival—a tribal philosophy of I-better-feed-this-kid-it-might-be-mine—there was also the belief that multiple ejaculations from different sources produced a sturdier child. My child would be made not of one man, but of the best in each of the men. I imagined on my child the long, sure legs of this man, the strange way he moved on land as if he belonged in water. I fancied that I could almost feel the working glide of his sperm, lean-legged swimmers racing through thick waters.

"I will be right out," I said pulling myself onto my knees, though it was sooner than I wanted to get up. But standing up off of his dirty bathroom floor felt good, and it felt good, too, the water on my eyes, and in my mouth, and the splash of water on my neck and water on my breasts. I would have wanted to keep going, cleaning myself, rinsing myself free of him or of what of him I could not use. But I needed to walk out there, into his room, say whatever I needed to say, in order to vanish.

My not knowing.

No charting basal temperature. No attempt to calculate ovulation. No checking under the microscope to see if the vaginal mucus was ferning. That was my decision after I gave up the donor bank. Just men. Selecting men without regard to a fertile time in the month. Particular and reckless without regard to possible danger. When a man reached into his pocket seeking the latex caution inside a square foil, I brought his hand back to my body saying, "No worry. I have it under control." I wanted at least enough men so that there could be no calculating backwards to recall a single face wrenched in the lost pleasure of his ejaculation. There would be no one face made loveliest to me as I proclaimed him father. Always more than one, two, or, better still, a blur of chosen male faces in the months I made a child.

And, just as I suppose that a hunter crouched at dawn, waiting to see the pricked-up antlers, the flicked white tail, must come to love the beast, I loved every one. The slant of a forehead, the bone structure of a face, a train of thought, the line of a man's calf. I was in the woods just outside the grazing herd. I was out there with hunger like a thrill through my body.

Nights, back in my empty rooms, I read about spiders and snakes, the mating practices of animals that were seldom tender. Even the lovely butterfly had less courtship than attack. I imagined the bright monarch in its pinned nightlong copulation. And then there were nights, a man's hand pressed against the small of my back, I was not the orange-vested hunter, but the beast, who too had killed, like every predator, with appetite and need.

The slope of shoulders. The open laugh and tilt of a chin. I saw the men for the boys they had been. I saw them for the way their faces might shift becoming the face of a girl.

I was not a hunter at all, I was at work as in a laboratory. The secret life. "You're something else," I remember a surgeon with blond curls saying. "Yes," I said giddy with my own secret, "I am something else."

The roofer told me as he entered me that he wanted a wife. He had kept one wife for a little while. "Now," he whispered, his mouth damp against my ear, "I want a wife for forever."

We were on a makeshift bed in his rambley, unfinished house. He had a face so beautiful I had made my selection seeing him walk up the aisle of the hardware store. He moved slowly trying to establish a rhythm with me.

I moved quickly.

"Slow down or you'll lose me," he whispered. "I want this to last. Let me give you more." His body was steady, easy, domestic.

He touched my hair, saying, "I'll take care of you," and "Yes, that's my baby." His hands slipped under to hold my ass. He pulled close so that I was forced to move with him. Slower, until we were not moving at all. "Yes," he said, "yes."

I said, "No. Let me show you something." Anything to get above him. First he held me below him, his hands snugging me up tightly against him. Then he let me turn him so that I sat on him. I posted up and down. The danger buzzer rang: fast, fast, get it and get away from this man fast.

"Slow it down, baby. You're going to lose me," he said.

"I need you in me," I whispered. "Please, let yourself be in me." I watched his eyes flicker shut, just little slits of white at the bottom. I watched his face as I lifted then lowered myself. His features each so exact they seemed to have a precise drawn outline.

He had been a wonderful choice.

After, he drifted, surfacing to whisper into my neck, "Baby, you took everything."

Fast. Fast. Get away fast.

I like men. Of course, I like men. Even now the idea of their mouths makes me swoon a bit. Mouths and the way men stand. I have always loved that classical lean stance, contrapposto. Sometimes with a man, I am less myself than Sybil's hand smoothing Marty's flyaway hair. I am Sybil cajoling Marty to dance when he brooded, saying to her that, surely, she might find a better man than he turned out to be. Mostly, and again I nod to Sybil, I like the wound of men. Their lack of completeness, some unwholesomeness that makes them like drifting wreckage in need of fixing.

So it was with pleasure I made my extensive efforts.

Should I go on? Should I say Henri was in a yellow room? That there was a taste to Brent's arms that I could not decide if I liked. Should I tell you there was one who threaded my hair through his fingers? And one who needed only for me to lick his lips for him to begin his finishing.

A man, with wide hips leaned into the wood bar. A frail man hunched by his drink. Nothing exceptional. There were no prospects. It had been a mistake, entirely foolish to look in a bar.

I felt someone come and stand next to me. I did not look. Despite everything I have said, despite my determined position, I am actually poorly suited to the task.

The simple truth is that I would rather be home reading.

"I hope you are looking for me," said the man standing next to me.

I was quiet. Who had caught me seeking? There was nothing I could think of to say. When I was ready, when I had collected myself, I tilted my head so that I could see him. A gem. Excellent blue eyes, teeth shining. A surprising find. I had not spotted him among the heap of the discardable.

"Yes," I said quietly turning my head back away. "Yes, I was hard at work looking for you."

It took a bit to prepare myself, to look at him directly, carefully. He was still smiling. Actually, a remarkable smile, a sneaky glint in his eye.

"And what were you looking for?" I asked trying to match his smile.

"Just this," he said.

"Just this?" I teased.

He looked a little stunned, but, I was pleased to see, recuperated quickly.

"Just everything," he said, moving closer so that our shoulders touched. "My name is . . ." but I didn't let him finish.

"No," I said, taking his hand, "no names."

"Whatever you say," he said, a quizzical broad smile. "You're in charge of the plan, honey."

"That is good," I said, "because there is quite a plan." I touched his arm then slid my hand over his thick wrist.

Of course I had no plan. Only the big plan to have a broth of the wondrous possible inside of me.

We stood for a bit—holding hands watching the bar—both of us, as it were, regrouping. Jazz was playing. We began lacing and unlacing fingers. At moments not exactly touching, then touching, barely, barely, barely touching.

"'Round Midnight,' Dollar Brand," he said, his finger lifted tapping out the music. I was again surprised, pleased.

"Your car? Where is it?" I asked as I guided us through the unlovely jumble of people filling the bar.

"It's a new car," he said quickly as if my going off with him was about his having a car. How, I have wondered, would he later describe it to an office confidant over coffee the next morning? That we got to his new car but never got inside the car? I would be described as single-minded in my efforts. That he was a little surprised to find I wore nothing, not even little string panties under my dress. That as he pressed into me, he had needed to steady himself and grasped the door handle for leverage. "She was half in the air, wedged between me and the car. You think I'm lying, don't you?" he might say. "For a long time after, she held me there. If I started to move, pull away, thinking she might want to get her feet back on the ground, she'd just clamp me in tight. Everything was real quiet between us. I tried a little talking. But there was no talking to this lady. Then she untangled her feet off of me and said, 'Thank you.'"

But would he finish off the story by admitting to his friend how long he waited, eyes closed, leaning against the car after I said, "I have just got to run into the ladies' room. Stay here. Rest till I return. Okay?"

Then I walked out of the lot, past the entrance to the restaurant, and down the few blocks to the bare room I rented.

No house. No husband. They would be the same, a distraction. All the time arranging hydrangea in jars on sills. Walls sponged with layers of pale blue and yellow paint. Even when he was not at home, I would find myself stopping to touch the chair back where he, the husband, had leaned his head. I can still see Sybil when I tromped inside for a snack. "Grab yourself a snack," she would say, not turning her head from the window where she stood waiting for the first sign of Marty.

It would not do for me to live like that.

I gave in when it came to the house. In the years

after leaving Marty and Sybil, I stayed in one lousy rental room after another until the moment I could not stand not making the room better. Then it was time to leave. One rental to the next rental. It was so easy leaving then. Then my life was what could fit in two suitcases and three cartons. It was books I had the hardest time leaving behind.

It would not do to raise the boy in rented basements or third-floor walk-ups. But I had forgotten the press of neighborhoods, the way the others needed everyone to belong. I was only thinking of how a child would suffer from drafty windows, from the landlady's stingy offerings of heat. But I was wrong.

Another rule: never bring a man to my rental room. Yet here I was walking up the back staircase with a man's hand curved around my ass as if he were weighing it.

"I do not live here," I said.

"Well, where are we going then?" he huffed. He spoke in bursts. I found his breathlessness entirely undesirable. He was a tall man, and, from what I could tell, strong. I had chosen him for what I perceived as a physical integrity and strength. Perhaps I had misjudged him.

Turning on the last stair, I took a look at him. "Would you rather not?"

"Yes, yes, I mean no, I mean, you have the key?"

Entering, I saw the room both as the man must have seen it, a room almost unlived in, the carefully made bed, the pictureless walls, the chair with a skirt thrown over its back. Stacks of books rising like small towers through the room.

He came up behind me and turned me toward him. I let myself consider for a last time if he was a correct choice. His vigor seemed to have returned. I decided he was adequate, if not my best specimen.

Then, soon enough, I suggested it was time for him to put on his clothes.

Now that he was one of the fathers, I found myself watching him even more closely. Straight shoulders, no round to his back. A lovely articulation around the pelvis. Extremely graceful in his lovemaking, and given his height this was a most surprising combination. I watched him dress. And, of all his qualities, perhaps this pleased me most, though I think it will perhaps sound strange—he put on his clothes well.

He had been most cooperative, really.

It took some effort for me not to thank him.

People make a great fuss about money and sex. Again, I believe, that is the mark of a poor imagination. Money, no doubt, has its uses, but I find it an altogether less engaging enterprise than even a second-rate history book. Granted, Sybil and Marty had been most generous in this regard. I imagined the effort it took them to conjure the note forwarded on after Sybil's death by the lawyer who, at their suggestion, still handles my finances. The note was practical. Even down to the last sentence. *Money notwithstanding, it would do well to find a passion.* If consistency is any sign of good parenting, than Sybil and Marty turned out to be winners in the end.

It was, actually, reading that letter when I first conceived, to use a most felicitous word, that I would have a child.

I had the image of reading a slim novel and, crooked next to me, touching my hair, was a child.

Nothing up till then had caught my heart with such a thrill. Not the book reviews I wrote for papers and periodicals, not the occasional history or science textbook that I was sent to index. The mistake Sybil and Marty had made was in the word *find*, which, at least in my case, showed far more effort and active direction. Instead, there it was, instant, magical, the child's damp fingers twirling my hair. I understood that about love one has little choice.

Later, in the neighborhood where I settled with Paul, the other mothers were always working to figure us out.

"Does he look like his dad?" a mother cautiously asked while we stood outside in the warm June evening, our children playing a last-before-bed game of chase.

Her voice thickened with concern, "And all on your own. I can't imagine how you do it."

I saw myself in that living-room doorway watching Sybil and Marty preoccupied in their nightly snuggles. And then I saw a tangle—head of dark curls, heard the resonant laugh.

"He looks like his dad," I said, forgetting for a moment the eager woman next to me. Our children were racing back and forth between trees. I motioned for Paul to come to me so that we might go inside. He ponied over and sprang up into my arms. He looked like his father. A boy, however, has more of a mother's genes operating in him. In fact, I was present, alive in every cell of his body. I kissed the top of his dark head.

"Is he nearby to help out?" the mother asked, all jangly with the possibility of her knowing something secret.

"Who? Who?" said Paul, ready to be part of our conversation.

"Nobody, Loverboy," I said, snuggling him close, the grassy smell clinging to him as I carried him into our house. "I promise, nobody at all."

Train

Like this waking in a white room, I woke in that white room, air blowing warm through white eyelet curtains, finely threaded, white sheets above and below me.

Everything in the room was white, a soft white, almost a transparency.

Here, all day, even at night, there is a glare.

There was a rectangle of light against the white wall and I half imagined or dreamed the rectangle was a door I might open and step through. I tried to imagine this was my white room of death and the train and the hospital and the man who called himself Jacob were my last fragmented moments, slivers of living memory that led me to this room. And yet, if this was my death, it was, I was certain, a wrong death, not the death I was meant for, and I understood then that for each person there might be many deaths, just as there are many possibilities, many chances with a life.

And yet, eventually I would stand up from the white

bed, open a real door, and walk out through rooms until I would find the room where somehow a man called Jacob waited for me

Old man on a train. How old? Who was this Jacob?

"Good day," he had said with a quick formal nod as he sat down in his seat across the train's aisle. And later, looking up from his book, "Will you join me in the dining car?" he asked. He nodded politely, clean and stiff in his suit when I declined with a terse, "No, thank you," my head hardly lifted from my book.

I was, according to the way gestation is calculated, almost ten weeks pregnant.

I had boarded a train to take me across the country. I looked forward to every minute on the train, to the splendor of reading while in motion, but, mostly, to the thrill of having hours and hours of imagining the child growing inside my body. Two weeks late. I could not help myself, I counted days. I purchased a kit. I did not need the test. But how I loved the science of it! As if already, truly, the child was a child of only my creation, my assiduous work in a laboratory. A drop of the first morning urine to stain the plastic wand blue or pink. Before the wand was pink, I began packing what few things I cared to keep.

My last rule: try to forget as much as possible about any of the circumstances. Yet, what kind of rule is that? To plan on forgetting? What a certain way to recall every detail.

I held the book in my lap but found, for the first time, I was too busy to read. I visualized the remarkable fingernail-sized body in its intricate makings, the spinal cord, the brain stem. By the tenth week, the inner portion of the ear was complete. The heart already formed and pumping. So many details that needed to be perfect. And in my imagining the beginnings of that new life with the child, I found myself slightly changing memories I had told myself I did not even have. I was making little shrines, places of obligation to each possible father in my heart.

Every town we passed through was a town where I might live with a child.

All landscapes were the landscape of this baby growing inside.

I stayed in my train seat, dozed, woke with low cramps.

I felt the man across the aisle looking at me. I felt pleased that I no longer needed to check what sort of man he might be, no longer needed to appraise him to see if he might be of use. But, anyway, I looked. Fine angled brow. He nodded his head. A purposeful, quick nod.

I was crossing the country, leaving the small city, riding east where I had more than six months to get the new life settled.

I was leaving the City of Fathers.

Six months was more time than I had ever given myself to set anything up before. Find the new City X where I might live. Or perhaps a town just outside a city where I would not rent but buy us a little house. A house with a good-sized yard. Our home together.

The cramps were not uncomfortable, they were really, at this point, like mild menstrual cramps.

I rose to make my way to the toilet.

Once inside, there was a rush, a flow, and a spot in the small metal train toilet. I put a square of paper to myself, looking for more blood.

The books indicated that even beyond the first trimester there might be spotting. Slight bleeding was possible all through a pregnancy. I wiped again. Nothing. Cautious, but not much alarmed, I returned to my seat. Out the window there were hours of farmed fields. Three hawks circled, dipping close to land and then lifting again. The fields gave way to more fields with choppy, short rows that zigzagged, as if set by a farmer tired by the predictable years and years of straight planting.

I am riding the train with my child. I returned to this over and over and it made seeing everything out the window—the hawks, the afternoon light laying stripes of light against the fields—it made all of it an exciting adventure.

Already I was saying to the child, "Look at that!"

I felt the man across the aisle still watching me.

They came on then, the searing cramps. I yanked my legs up close to my chest. Soon there was no sitting still and I walked the narrow train aisle, jostling through cars at first purposefully as though I were looking for someone. But then just pacing, stopping when the cramping bunched inside me. I sat back in my seat, trying to focus out the window. But I needed to shut my eyes against any shifts in light. Then there was a sudden hemorrhage of blood, and standing up from the train seat I saw there was no longer any possibility of discretion. There was no hiding the blood on the seat cushion, on my skirt and legs. Then the jostle and a sense that I might faint and the man in his country suit suddenly appearing at my side saying, "I've got you. You're okay."

How was it that he lifted me from the train with his old-man arms? He did not leave me once in the hours after I was off the train when my body seized and I rocked with pain that branched through me. He wiped my forehead with a rough pocket cloth.

I heard the sureness of a voice shouting, "I demand you give this woman something."

There were rooms with lights and, in a dark room, machines that beeped and made pinching sounds. All the time, the man was there, always holding some part of me—my leg, my hand, his face close to my face saying, "I have gotten them to give you another shot of it. You'll feel much better now." His face, thick creases by his eyes, and how, as I drifted shifting deeper into some hollow of pain, he seemed to me less a man and more an angel. And I wanted to say, "How does an angel have an old man's beard?" But I could not find words, and when I found words I could not make any sounds, or the sounds I brought forth were all wrong.

But what if I was wrong? What if I opened the door to find no man?

I had been on a train. Then I was not on a train. And then there was the white room.

I touched my body. Everything was exactly as I re-membered. What did I remember? First hours looking out the window. Farms, golden swatches of planted fields. Flat land, and in the distance, planted trees and a house circled by sheds and barns. More fields.

Was it in the car or at the counters where they asked for my name and where I lived and his voice rose with a sharp anger: "Can't you see, she can't speak"? Or was it later in the rooms of the hospital that he leaned in and said, "My name is Jacob. I've taken care of everything."

Did I know at once when I heard a woman scream, a squall of a woman's voice, "I want my baby. Give me back my baby"? Or was it later when the woman had screamed herself hoarse and was still pleading in pitiful raspy shouts for her baby, that I suddenly heard the voice and understood that I was the woman who had lost her child.

He Had Been There

He had been there. In the white room. And only during times while I had slept so that I never heard him in his comings, he left trays of thick vegetable soup and dark-grained bread, dishes of minty rice and sauces with flavors that woke me. I did not want to be hungry but I ate everything he left. I slept, sweaty dreamless sleeps, sheet-wrapping, tousled sleeps. Then again I was waking exhausted, as if I had never slept, waking with strange smells that jolted my hunger. Leave, I commanded myself. Get up. But instead I ate and, before the end of the last bowl, was again asleep.

How many bowls of minted rice were brought to me before I stood up and opened the white door? I walked out of the white room down the hallway with its three closed doors to a kitchen. I tried to remember the face of the man whose back was toward me. I could try and leave. There was time to slip back down the hallway before he sensed my presence.

"Oh," he said, turning around. He stood and went to a doorless cupboard and took a napkin from a small stack of folded napkins. "I've just been waiting for dinner," he said, glancing to the set table. Then I saw that the kitchen table was set for two and I understood that he knew that I was leaving the bed before I had stood up from it. "Please, of course you'll join me, you must be quite hungry."

For days, was it days? how many days? I watched Jacob in his kitchen. He moved deliberately, without a single excessive gesture, peeling and mincing cloves of garlic, slicing open and pitting lemons, cutting the thin membranous skin from oranges. Watching a man who moves knowingly through a kitchen slays me. He gathered mint and parsley into bowls, wiped down the wide wooden cutting board with a strong sweep of a wet cloth.

Each morning I woke and thought, Today I will leave this stranger's house. And then I would walk out to the kitchen and forget about leaving.

He leaned against the counter, a paring knife lifted absently in his hand. "You must take great care during your recuperation to only let the purest things into your body." He looked past me, and I was afraid to follow his gaze for what I might find behind me. Then his back was to me, and I watched the flicking muscles in his back, the small movements of his neck as he peeled, then began slicing, potatoes.

He stopped working, his knife anchored into the

spiny back of a pineapple as if there could be no divid-
ing efforts and each took his entire concentration.

"This morning," he said, " I found myself thinking of
Virgil. It is time, I suppose, to read *The Georgics* again.

He asked questions phrased as answers. "You've
read Virgil's *Georgics?*"

"You don't mind a little citrus flavor to your salad?"
he asked, arranging orange slices in a fan against the
green leaves.

He set the potatoes into a glass bowl of water. He
wiped his hands and picked up a longer knife.

"You know, when the Spanish first introduced the
potato to Europeans it was blamed for regional out-
breaks of leprosy and tuberculosis?"

Jacob poured coffee from a glass pot asking,"Who
used the phrase 'single father' back when I was making
lunches each morning?"

"No matter how big your child is," Jacob said, suddenly looking too tired to hold the coffeepot, "there are
some things about his own mother he need never
know."

"This was my wife," Jacob said holding open a carton crammed with pictures, a spill of black and whites,
all of a woman, her face like a full throbbing heart or
was it some wild animal, quick eyes and desperate dark
beauty? In one picture a boy holding his mother's face
between his two small hands.

"Who could hold a son back from wanting to understand his own mother, for Christ's sake. His own beautiful mother working so hard to die," Jacob said. But

feeling the sting of his son Isaac's anger was another story. Even with all the preparation, hard for a father not to raise a voice back. Tell him how how it really was—the potions and cures, the promises of doctors who couldn't help but fall in love with her. The vials she would drift home with.

Jacob laughed and said, "But I knew he was a good boy. His name? Exactly! Isaac, son of Jacob. And why the hell not! I suppose I was thinking of Wordsworth. 'The child is the father of man.' "

"You have read Emerson?" Jacob asked abruptly.

Suddenly, I could not breathe. Now he was standing at the sink, his back to me.

"That's not fair of me. I saw the Emerson in your bag when I was looking for any papers that might help me. I was astonished. Emerson! Who reads Emerson on a train these days? My God, who reads Emerson at all these days?"

He turned the cold faucet and, one by one, rinsed chicken pieces, patting them dry, rubbing lemon over the pebbly leg and breast skin.

I wanted to say, "Please, stop." But I said nothing and shook my head though his back was toward me.

"Anyway, seeing the Emerson made me recall how just fourteen months after his wife's death—she died, you must know this, of tuberculosis. Anyway, Emerson went out one day and dug her up. It horrifies most people. How could he do this? Dig her up? Surely a sign that he was unwell. That Emerson not only dug up her coffin, but that he opened it. Many years later he did the same with his young son, Waldo. There is nothing strange about this to me. It is not only grief, you understand, I think you must understand, he had to see for himself what his young wife had become."

I needed to get out of this house. I had boarded a train carrying a child. Everything clean, no man years later at a door saying, "I want to spend some time with my child." But I had passed the child out, a small thickness of tissue and blood in some hospital toilet. Beds, floors, in parking lots against cars—I had gone about it all wrong. I needed to get out. "I have to go," I said, but when I stood and tried to take a step, I crumpled and heard Jacob say, "I've got you."

"What do you need?" he asked later, kneeling by the bed in his old man's suit.

I had always known what I needed. Now I had no idea what I needed. Before me was an angel who would fix me dishes and bring me books.

"Can you stay?" he asked, turning away from me so that I knew I did not need to answer.

Do Not Promise

Trains, trains, benches where I slept when the station master was kind or drunk and dozed-out behind a gated booth. Or I arrived sleepless and frayed into the center of cities. "Then I will have the suite," I said, leaning against the polished front desk of a first-class hotel when the concierge snarled that no standard was available. Days where what passed were ripped-away towns where men and women did not bother to look up when a train went through. Then I let the gleaming doorman hold open heavy, carved doors while I carried shopping bags. I recrossed over both sides of my shadow. I got out at the thirteenth floor. I hung a Do Not Disturb sign and stayed up watching the wall for two days straight. I got on the number 5. I slept in a ravine. I stood in a marble shower. I walked in shoes not meant for walking into parts of a city where people hung from windows and by night there were no sidewalks.

I boarded the North Line.

I had no life to leave on the South Pier.

Paul, there is a man with your dark curls who said, "Don't promise me what I will ask you to promise."

I had no plan. I had lost my plans in stations where the conductor said, "Miss, you don't belong here." All I had left was a letter from Sybil and Marty's lawyer. I had money. *Does he look like his dad? He sprang up into my arms.* I thought I had nothing left in me to lose.

"You don't look like you belong here," a man riding the elevator said.

"Excuse me?" I angled myself away from conversation. But I was ready to fight.

I got out on the thirteenth floor. The man got out, too. Kept in step with me.

The man said, "You are not wearing a name tag."

I stopped short in the narrow hotel hallway, sneered, "Oh, really? Forgive me. I did not understand that one must identify oneself with name tags to stay in your ridiculous approximation of a first-class hotel."

He was laughing, shaking his mane of dark curls, reaching out, touching my arm, and even as I recoiled from the gesture, he was still laughing. "No, God," he was talking between breaths of laughter, big abandoned laughter, riveting to watch. His full lips moved as if he were making a song when he said, "I'm with the convention, Futures Industry. Sorry. Really. I just assumed you were a trader with one of the regional houses."

I backed up, my head knocking against a wall

sconce. "You are not with the hotel?" I asked, immediately regretting having asked.

"What? You thought I was hotel security? That's splendid. Now we're even." The extraordinary surge, the power of his laugh was frightening. I turned, walked close to the wall toward my room.

"If I said I was the hotel security," he said catching up, "you would have to say yes if I asked you to follow me."

The key slid into the lock. I turned on it until the door opened. "No, I would simply pay my bill and get far away from this low-class place," I said slipping inside my room and locking the door.

Inside the hotel room, I looked through my new purchases, triangles of silk and dresses cut on the bias. I took out my suitcase and began packing. The phone rang. "I'm sorry," a man's voice said. "My name is Paul."

I said nothing. I held a slip dress up in one hand, the light textured through it.

"Please, I don't really know what I'm doing," the man called Paul continued. "I don't know why I'm even on the phone. Of course this is crazy. This is crazy, calling you. If not dinner, a drink. If not a drink, a ride up to the lake. At least save me from a night of convention torture," he said.

"I am not in the saving business," I said, letting the dress drop.

So, yes Paul, this is, as I promised, the second story. But of that night, what exactly do I remember? Too little, I am afraid. Or the wrong things. That the walls of the room were a horrid shade of green and that it seemed strange to laugh in a green room. Although laughing was not anything I was used to, it seemed utterly familiar to lie on the bed, Paul's and my legs angled against the walls, laughing till we folded up with cramps.

I was dismantled. I was without determination. For the first time it was I who was stunned.

As best as I can remember, it was as I first told you. That night he was Odysseus, the disguise off and come home to our carved bed. And when I whispered, "Show me," like weather he moved over me, warm fog, a Berg wind, sudden breeze and lull. "Show me," I whispered, and I was shown narrow, burr-ridden paths that opened onto tented markets where baskets of olives and baskets of hands were loaded on the backs of dogs and camels and men. I was taken into the temples of spruce and fir and heard the singing dirt and a skid of rocks. When I lifted to watch us, Paul was watching, his eyes wet. "Don't promise what I will ask you to promise," Paul said, closing his eyes.

You are the story of bodies, ours, the perfect fit of them, the spill of each other on the thirteenth floor in a room with green walls. You are the story of one night, purposeless and extreme, the holy combustion of a woman and man unprepared for what they have been delivered unto.

He said, "For years, happily, I have been married. And now, what is this? Really, I understand that you have no reason to believe that this, or anything like this, is nothing I've ever done before."

He said, "Even still, I've been waiting for this. Whatever happens, you must please know that you are the one true love of my life."

In the morning, pinning on his convention name tag, he flattened his hand like a pledge over the tag, and said, "I leave after the first meeting. Promise me you will forget this, even my name."

"Sure," I said, billowing the sheet into a parachute. "I have my rip cord pulled already."

But we had stopped by then being able to laugh.

We held each other, trying to say whatever few things might keep us together in the room a little longer.

He was not Odysseus, nor a god come out of the reedy banks. I saw he was a lonely man in a suit speaking to a woman in a green room on the thirteenth floor. We stood upright a little longer. Then he was gone.

Later, after more towns, I was certain and amazed there was a child, a new child was growing inside of me. What about the equation? I had been wrong. You were the keeper child. A child of passion. No promise could keep this passion child from me. And I knew that what grew in me would have to be a son. I named you then, Paul, the right child, my loverboy.

PART THREE

He Is Ours, Lady

Licorice

He holds out his arms, wrists crossed. "Tie me up," he says. We are stopped at a street corner. For the last half an hour, I watched while he considered each jar of brightly colored gummy bears and sharks, the sour sugar discs, chocolate malt balls and yogurt-covered raisins. No coaxing I could do could get him to hurry up. Back and forth in his silent evaluation, until he pointed to a snarl of three-foot lengths of red licorice. "I would like this, please," he said.

Now he jerks his slender wrists. "Tie me up."

Cars stop at the red light. "Cross, Honey," I say, holding his elbow and stepping into the street.

"No," he resists. "I want to do this here."

"Here?" But there is no arguing.

The licorice ropes twice around his wrists, knots bulky with a chunky double knot. He looks down grinning, then backs away from me.

"Ladies and Gentleman," he says. Who can resist

this little impresario, lifting his arms, wrists bound in red candy?

"Behold Ladies and Gentleman, as I eat my way to freedom," he shouts, and with a quick bow to me and then a bow to the idling cars at the red light, he begins gnawing his way out.

Real School

I never wanted to send him off.

I did not have to go on visits to see just how it would be. The bright-eyed teachers with their credentialed activities. Their professional encouragement: "Yes, he's fine in two seconds after you are out the door." Their update notes sent home in lunch boxes. I could not sit eagerly at conferences to be told about my child. His age-appropriate progress. I would be compelled to ask, Can you recognize Manet's *Déjeuner sur l'herbe* or Bach's Cantata no. 7? They will discuss his willingness to be part of the group, which mostly seems to me to be a nice way of saying that he needs to share infections with other boys and girls. He needs to spend his day with the ones with glazed fevered eyes, the I'm-sure-Johnny-just-ate-something-funny-last-night vomiters, the pink-eyed weepy ones asleep by snack time. Even Dr. Spock, whom I quite admire, he says it, too. He claims, in fact, that this is the main lesson in school. Not the ABC learning.

Not how to hold the pencil and write your name. *The main lesson,* claims Spock, *is how to get along with the rest of the world.*

I am not interested.

Put us on our kitchen floor with a bunch of plastic containers and a pot of water, the Brandenburg Concertos as our water music. We are fine.

"But who will Paul play with when the other kids are in kindergarten?" asked Marianne, a mother from across the street. She had the self-appointed voice of every do-gooder. She fanned herself with the kindergarten application she had brought over.

We stood watching the children play a game of tag. In that low golden light, the other children looked almost as perfect as he looked. How horrible for a mother of more than one. Always needing to find balance—or to harbor secret preferences. Or worse, to give up and stare with blurry equality at all the children.

"We will be fine," I said.

"But he needs other children. You should see how they grow and mature, even in the preschool," she said emphatically.

The children ran in swarms. The younger children seemed to be having trouble understanding who was It. Mostly they all ran about the lawns pushing and tagging and every child shrieking, "You're It!"

"We do fine together." I tried to sound friendly.

"Well, you owe it to yourself to at least go down and

have a look at the school. Sign him up just in case you change your mind."

The tagging had turned to pushing. The swarms were in toppled bunches. Teams were forming.

"Really, this is what is best for us," I said.

Marianne winced, annoyed, defeated. "Who do you think you are?" she snapped. "Dr. Spock?"

We were fine.

Every day was a day of our making. We stayed inside on rainy days, the table a jumble of glued sticks and painted sticks. We built tall towers using boxes and cans from the pantry, the wonderful rounded shapes of spice jars crowning the spires. Or out we went into rain, pretending we were potters crafting pinch pots from the thick wet clay that collected in the mud we dug. And when the sun broke through we let the mud dry on our feet to a hard flaky crust.

Other days we left our streets and wandered to streets where the food in store windows was unnameable to us. We tried everything with points and nods, saying to the aproned woman, "Yes, yes, a bit of that, too." Then we sat at the feast. Paul made his list of favorites, making up names for each dish, and then days later, looking up from his drawing, he said, "My Miss Mama, I am starving for *soongaloongabobo.*"

"I was just craving the very same," I said, and we would both hurry to clean up our paints and wash our brushes and get down to the shop where the lady with crooked teeth scooped us helpings of *soongaloonga-bobo,* and pointed to a bowl of something spiky green and said, "Try. Very fresh. So good."

If we found a spider in the kitchen window, we read about spiders. Looked at the Anansi Spider Folk Tales. Began spider dioramas and research.

Did she know, Paul asked the town librarian, that daddy longlegs resemble spiders but are not spiders?

She raised her eyebrows and said, in the horrid way adults speak to children, "Really?"

"Yes," said Paul ready to get on to his important finding of the morning. "And do you know daddy long-legs have penises and spiders do not have penises?"

The librarian reorganized her face. "You sure have a live one on your hands," she said to me with a tight, concerned smile.

"No, it is true," Paul insisted, putting *The Audubon Society Field Guide to North American Insects and Spiders* on her counter, "We read it in this book, which I would like to check out."

I looked to see if the librarian was prepared to let herself be educated. But she was slightly horrified, I could see, at the possibility of people actually handling books in her library.

We read everything. A book of maps. *Complete Fairy Tales of the Brothers Grimm.* An origami book. There was no section of the library where we did not browse.

Days of all-day in the library, cozied-up on the sofa or on the worn library chairs, we read books. We stretched out on the floor of the stacks admiring the perfect face of

Michelangelo's Delphic Sibyl. There was no question of appropriate and inappropriate books. There were only the books we loved and the books we had yet to love. In a snowbound week at home, we piled books higher and higher, until, at the end of the week, we could measure Paul's height against a tower of books.

We stayed in our rapture of learning through the year the other neighborhood children scribbled and pasted and sniffled their way through kindergarten.

First Grade

In comes the doctor. In comes the nurse. In comes the lady with the alligator purse. Measles, says the doctor. Mumps, says the nurse. Chicken Pox, says the lady with the alligator purse.

"When do I get to go to school?" he asked. It was morning and he had been quietly working on making a potion in a plastic beaker.

"Never," I jumped. My tone must have been scolding, forbidding enough to shame him and make him desperate for school at the same time.

I tried to backpedal: "They make you sit at desks all day."

"So what?" he said. "That is easy. I can do that."

He was right. I was sinking in my own stupid responses. It was ridiculous that I had not planned for this set of questions. But it is always that way, I think. It is almost a pathetic joke. All the careful thinking

about the big questions—Sex, Death, God, Whatever—
the careful, heart-to-heart conversations planned out
for the perfect moment. And the child looks up as a
waitress is asking for your lunch order and he says, "Is
it God or the mother that makes you have a penis or a
vagina?" And you are left staring up at the frazzled
waitress, saying, "Dear, did you want grilled cheese or
tuna fish?"

"You cannot make potions in school," I said.

He poured the soapy, green liquid from the plastic
beaker into the bowl. "That is fine. I will make potions
after school. I want to go on the bus," he said.

"Today we can take a bus if you like," I said, sounding cheery.

"No, not a bus with you." He looked at me, con-
fused with what he knew was feigned ignorance on my
part. "I mean the yellow children's bus," he said, stirring the bubbles with a chopstick.

"Perhaps sometime," I said.

For a week, maybe two, he let it drop. But then he
was at me full speed. He had learned in that time—
where and when I have no idea—that the other children
in the neighborhood went to school. When was he
going? he demanded. He wanted to go, and did I know
that kids younger than him were already going to
school?

I tried a new tactic. He was already at school. This
was school, I announced. Home School. Lots of kids did
Home School. It was the way it was done in the time of

his heroes. Did he think Daniel Boone or Michelangelo spent their days in school? Anyway, I said, the children in school did not yet know how to read and he would find it boring reciting A-B-C until he was allowed to come home.

This was not school, he argued. This was home.

"Do they do that in Real School?" he asked when I told him to lie down for a nap.

When I set us up with water and brushes he asked, "Do they paint in Real School?"

And I made the mistake of answering truthfully, "Yes, I suppose they paint in all schools."

We were outside playing Red Light Green Light when he shouted to Marianne. "Excuse me," he called. "I need to ask you a question."

She waved and started to get into her car.

He took off running, charging across the street. Marianne and I both shrieked at the sight of him charging full force into the road. But he did not stop at the sound of us. And on the other side of the road, he marched right across Marianne's lawn. She hurried toward him. I watched in a panic as they talked in her driveway. He had never done that. Just sprung away from me and not listened when I called out to him. She spoke eagerly, her hands moving above Paul's head. He kept nodding and nodding and I thought he looked as if his head were attached to a cord she kept pulling. They walked over to our yard together. She made an exaggerated point of stopping on the empty road, looking both ways, saying, "Okay, now," to him as they stepped off the curb.

"Thanks," I said, grabbing his arm when he was in reach.

"Paul has apologized for scaring us, for doing something he knew was dangerous like running across the street. But all he wanted to know was how to sign up for school," Marianne said, practically drooling with delight over her own words. "He wants me to tell you that all you have to do is go over and fill out the school form and then Paul can go to school."

"Thanks," I said not looking at her but at Paul. "Do you understand what you just did?"

"I think he's just so excited about the chance to go to school," she said in a drawl of success. Looking at Paul she said, "How wonderful! A boy who really wants to learn." Her face was triumphant. She could not wait to have my son where all the neighbors believed he belonged.

"A little excitement is a great thing," I said, matching her phony voice. "But I think it is a good idea for a child to first learn at home how to properly cross the road."

"Paul," she said, refusing to meet my snarl. She bent close to him, taking his hands as if making some agreement. "Every child can go to school and ride the yellow bus. You just need to tell your mother to bring you over to the elementary school tomorrow and she'll sign you up to be with the other children. They are having so much fun."

"Magically," he announced the night before he began school, "I will cover my eyes and when I open them, I will be gone."

Shack

The woman said on the phone, "Really, don't think house. Think shack."

I was not thinking house. I was thinking about the wooden steps she described leading steeply down to the beach, hibiscus and poison ivy matted against the sand dunes. Up and down those steep stairs, two weeks of sandwiches and squat folding chairs and books with pages stiffened by salt water. There would be separate trips to carry tubes and rafts. Stepping carefully on the wobbly board close to the bottom, we would jump the last step with its rotted-out strippy wood. At night we would check each other for rashes and ticks. Wake early to explore the tidal flats.

I needed to get us far away.

"Look, I'll warn you," she said, her voice sounded gnarled by the elements, "even though it's not technically an island, at high tide our little bridge is impassable. For that time you're stranded on the point. If you want to go to town, you've got to know you want to go to town. I mean you've got to plan your day a little or you'll find there's nothing you can do about it, you're stuck at the beach house. We're used to it. But I'll tell you, there are some renters who feel like prisoners when they're cut off from the mainland."

I said, "That sounds lovely."

We drove at night. The drive seemed hardly long enough, though it was more than five hours from our house to the beach. I wished that night that I could keep driving, crossing highways to small local routes, driving with Paul sleeping in the backseat of the car. I should never go back to the house. It could be left like all the other homes I had left. A life in our car, driving back and forth across the county, staying in towns a month or two, visiting all the town libraries in America. We would stay just long enough to read the town's history, invariably reading about those who had left the little town, gone off to big cities, made money, discoveries, and now the town claimed them as their own—boys who might any minute return and come for milk to the supermarket. I thought with comfort about the rooms we might rent for a few nights, the mild, "Where you heading?" "Where you been?" questions of motel women who only left town for doctor visits.

If he asked, I could tell Paul that school buses and schools were not in this new part of the country. But the thrill of that plan did not last long. I slowed and let cars speed past. I had raised him to look, I had told him to examine everything. There was no hiding the world from Paul.

I felt dizzy.

A car honked and, just in time, I swerved.

"Door'll be open," she said over the phone. The shack, Jeanette explained, had come in the mail, an original 1920s Sears and Roebuck mail-order house. It was a marvelous idea, the pieces arriving, a whole house miraculously fitting in the mailbox. She would be in town that day we arrived, she explained, doing a big shop for herself. Would I like her to fill up the fridge so I would not need to bother with town for a few days? What did the child eat for breakfast? When I said no, it was not necessary, she said, "Look, I'll pick up a carton of milk and some cereal for you, so at least there's something for morning. Otherwise you'll start out all wrong. Listen, high tide's at 7:37, so you're out of luck if you wait."

A plate of home-baked blueberry muffins was on the kitchen counter when I carried in the first load of bags.

It was a perfect shack, a charming wreck of a place. No plastic lobsters tacked on the walls. No draped fishing buoys and nets. Instead, washed cotton muslin covering the old couch. To celebrate, I ate a muffin in two bites, the berries fresh and bursting.

Paul was awake when I got back out to the car. "Is this the beach?"

"Go back to sleep, Lovey," I said. "You can see everything in the morning. Let me carry you to bed."

"I want to go to the beach," he said, and I thought

for a moment that he was actually asleep, just having opened his eyes momentarily.

"Tomorrow, Love," I said, lifting him from the car.

He squirmed with such determination that I had to set him on the ground. "Hey, what is going on, Sleepy?" I asked, my eyes stinging from all the driving.

"We came to the beach, we should go to the beach."

"Okay, okay, but just a quick look. It is the middle of the night, Kiddo," I said, laughing.

Around the back side of the house, we were hit with a slap of wind. He grabbed for my hand. "Hold on," I said. "It is dark."

Of course, he could see it was dark, but my saying it seemed to make him grasp tighter. I liked that, his tight hold on my hand. He was lit by the inside light from the shack and his amazement was extraordinary. His astonishment, his fear and anticipation, his clear understanding that we were standing in the midst of extraordinary power—the wind, the dark crashing sounds of the ocean below us.

"Do not look back at the house," I leaned over and said to him.

Of course, he immediately looked back at the house and then back at me. "Why? Why?" he shouted, trying to figure out what I was hiding. "Why can I not look at it?" he tugged at my hand.

"Because." I lifted him up in my arms and he wrapped his arms around me and pulled his face in close to my body. "Because out there is the magic world. You must first make your magic wish and then I will show you this wonderful house."

He was quiet for what seemed a very long minute. The wind stung against my face in a way that I found entirely pleasing. I had been wrong. I wanted the ride to go on forever. But we had come to this perfect place with the warm wind, a flowery and salty smell, the toss of stars overhead, and my boy pressed close to me. Everything was possible again. Every night we might come out to the beach until we had learned the shapes of the night sky.

He would decide he did not want to go off on the yellow bus. I could stop being afraid.

As if he had thought the same thoughts, he kissed my cheek.

"We can go in now," he said in a grave and quiet tone. "What did you wish?"

"What I always wish. I wished that we would always be together. Loverboy and his Miss Darling. And you? What was your wish?"

"I cannot tell you," he said hugging me tightly. "If I tell you, it will never, never come true."

All the houses on the point were essentially shacks, built mostly as makeshift extensions by grandchildren and then great-grandchildren, outbuildings from the one large cliff house. Over the years, the children's grandchildren came with kids. A few had sold off their shacks. Our Sears and Roebuck mail order was one summer's project of a particularly wild Uncle Bill. He had not had any offspring. Dead years later in some remote mountain village in Ecuador, it took two years for the family to even learn Uncle Bill was dead. And then, for the next ten years, everyone in the family was half expecting a whole Ecuadoran village might arrive to claim the shack.

We learned all this the first morning at the beach.

And we learned that we were the only summer renters, the new blood for a whole island of people who had bored one another a generation ago and were still stuck keeping one another summer company.

"You'll come for drinks tonight?" Jeanette asked, plopping down next to my beach chair. She had her gray hair piled in a thick sprawling bun on top of her head. She spoke with a wagging metronome-like head motion so that I kept waiting for her hair to shake itself out of the bun. It was obvious there was no saying no, so I asked, "What can we bring?"

"For tonight just yourselves and whatever juicy gossip you'll let us pry out of you after a couple few drinks." She had a great whoop of a laugh which she let out like random punctuation, her head stopping its wag for a split second. "Martini okay?"

"Sounds like with you I better stick to water," I said, inspiring Jeanette to send up a few short whoops loud enough for Paul to turn and call out, "What, Mama?"

"Divorced? Right?" she said, looking out to where Paul kneeled at the tide back at his morning production of dripping wet sand cast into slippy spires.

"Forget it!" I said, already light-headed. "I am waiting for my first martini, Jeanette, before I say the least little thing to you."

The island cottages were owned by a sprawling clan of ne'er-do-wells, the dwindling last fortunes, sober uncles who went on February benders, grown children who were not speaking to a daffy aunt. They were picture-perfect to the island. Every tousled one of them out shingling a roof or banging new clapboard on their cottages. Everyone offered their remedy for dune erosion. The constant corrosive salt spray. Island stories. The year the September hurricane took down Eddie's house. The summer the blueberry bushes were coated in some odd mold. Every cousin, aunt, and brother ready to confide to Paul and myself a little piece of the family history. Worn generations, they were as much a part of the landscape as the beach glass Paul and I went out to collect at low tide.

I picked out the olive from the martini and passed myself off as just another run-of-the-mill single mother. That there was no ugly divorce, insane lover, or nasty father in the wings of Paul's and my life satisfied them quickly. More time for them to tell us about the weird saps and nuts Uncle Bill used to send back for Christmas, or poor Eddie's luck, or the way PopPop and Nannie had, in their last years, taken to talking to each other in Pig Latin.

Paul and I were delighted, a kooky storybook come alive. And at night, back from a clambake, instead of our bedtime book, we tried to remember who was related to whom and through which branch.

What was not to love? Rose Hibiscus, dunes trellised in fuschia flowers, someone coming by the house with fresh live lobsters, Paul and I ferried out at sunset in a wooden sailing rig?

What was not to love? I was a renter once again. Paul had not mentioned school once. Together we were studying the summer night sky. Perseus, Andromeda, the Dipper tipped, and the Milky Way was a thick chewy band we reached to touch.

He woke in his sandy bed and came to me where I drank my coffee on the wooden deck, saying, "My Miss Mama, I just love you. Can we go back to the beach today?"

I laughed, pulling his warm sleepy body up on my lap. It made me laugh the way he half expected the beach to be gone each morning, or that I might sweep us away from the beach, drive us into town for some ungodly reason. We loved being stranded, cut off at high tide. We walked to the narrow wood bridge to watch the sand road wash over until eventually only the highest planks of the arched bridge could be seen. At low tide we collected hermit crabs in pails.

A week had passed. We had not worn shoes.

Evenings we walked over to one shack or another for drinks. Drinks turned to dinner. The bass were running strong and Jeanette had a way with bluefish. Uncle Pete gave Paul a hammer, nails, and a small saw and, while the grown-ups drank, Paul worked on a driftwood town.

"You're a good mom," Pete said leaning against the porch rail.

"I try," I said, trying not to be pleased with the compliment.

"No, really," he said. "Most moms would be all over their kid about careful this and careful that with the nails. Hard for most kids to have a second of fun."

"That is the least of my worries," I joked. "We have been using a hammer since he could walk."

"Well, in that case, I've got a whole mess of work for the boy." Pete gave a shake and caught himself when the whole rail leaned like it might promptly give out.

We were so happy that I thought we should stay on after the two weeks, maybe keep him hammering his driftwood town until it got too cold. No yellow bus crossing the washed-out bridge. Stay and watch the whales offshore in the fall. Sleep in flannel and socks and even caps to keep in the heat. And if it got too cold, too unbearable in that mail-order shack, we would pack our things and in a gale wind drive off the point. Just start driving. Maybe out west. Maybe out to see the Grand Canyon.

It was Thursday when he started.

"We leave on Saturday," he announced to me. We were sitting out on the beach stairs; I was trying to show him the W of Cassiopeia.

"Well, maybe not. I spoke to Jeanette," I said. "Maybe we will stay on for a while. Stretch summer out a little longer."

He stood up and started up the stairs.

"Hey, where are you going, Kiddo?"

"To tell Jeanette we cannot stay. We have seventeen days left of summer." He was speaking in a breathless rush. A wind had come up and it made him hard to hear.

"Slow down, Kiddo. We are fine. Come back here before it gets too windy. If you tilt your head a little more, the W will pop up at you."

"School," he shouted, but despite his shouting I had the feeling he was not speaking to me. "I have school. I have to go to school."

He turned and slammed into the screen door. Then, before I could help him, he disappeared into the shack. I stood up and followed him in. His shorts and T-shirt were left in a pile. He was in bed, his blankets yanked stubbornly up to his chin.

Uncle Pete came by. "Paul's been asking to come out for some fishing." Paul's face sparked with excitement. When had Paul asked? It disturbed me not to know.

"I do not think today will work," I said. "We have to get ourselves into town before the bridge is washed over."

"It's fine. Let the boy stay with me. Give you a chance to get the shopping done with a little peace of mind." And then, as if he was covering all the bases, he struck a sailor's salute. "The boy will keep his life jacket on. Promise, madame. Besides I've only thrown overboard two children and they were both fish-food size."

Paul laughed looking at Pete. He was already in a thrall.

"Can I do the fishing?" he begged. "Will we catch something really big?"

"I do not think so, Pete. Thank you so for the offer. Another day would be great," I said.

"Come on, Mama, please, please, please," Paul said, pressing his hands together in a pose straight out of his library foray among medieval paintings.

Pete caricatured the pose. "Yeah, Mom, please, please, please. Let the kid catch a fish," he said, opening his hands as if he were making an offering.

"I had better come."

But Pete cast a wrinkle-nosed look to Paul. "What do you think, kid, do we want a mom aboard?"

"Nah," said Paul, his voice full of big-boy nonchalance but squirming right up and giving me a tight hug. "I promise I will listen to Pete."

Pete gave a whoop, clearly the call of their entire clan. "You better, mister, or you'll be fish food in a quick splash. We'll be out about three hours, I'll see how it goes." He winked at Paul. "Depends how soon we catch ourselves a mermaid, right?"

There was no saying no without a major tiff with Pete. It occurred to me that I might use the fishing to negotiate a new equation. Seeing Paul standing beside Pete, I began thinking that I would need to show Paul that we had just begun learning about islands. And like any of our inquiries, we needed to be thorough. There might be months of study ahead of us, marking changes on the winter beach, watching the migration of whales and birds. Fishing.

"I'll have some clam chowder waiting for you," I said, forcing a smile, "but remember, you two fishermen, absolutely no taking the life vest off." I looked at Pete. Gave him my serious do-not-mess-a-minute-with-my-son's-safety look. He smiled boyishly, gave me his I-am-bad-but-I-can-be-good-too look.

It was only then that I realized I had missed it. The whole thing was for me. All of his attention, his chumming with the boy, it was all attention to me. I had missed the entire exchange. Now I saw him all over again—how he had arrived for cocktails the last few nights showered and in a clean, unpressed linen shirt. I was out of practice. It was me he was after. If he could pal up with Paul, I might trust him, might find him someone to notice. Jeanette, the whole island—even dead Uncle Eddie—they were all rooting for him, coaching him that the way to my single mother's heart was through the kid.

"And hopefully the men will have some fish to bring in for supper," he said, putting an arm around Paul.

I drove in a rush to town, shopped, grabbing everything, enough provisions to make it through October, though we only had till Saturday at the shack. The grocery store was thick with vacation families, fathers trying to make an August adventure of every aisle, and lobster red mothers depressed to be vacationing and in the cereal aisle. Their carts were filled with babies and bad food.

The checkout girl moved glacially, her bangles ringing against her tan arms each time she scanned an item. And she had to curl her long bangs behind her ear after almost every item. I stood in line behind a family with two overstuffed carts.

Paul was not with me. What had I done? I had lost my mind. Paul was on a boat with a man who, as far as I knew, knew how to do only two things: roof his house and drink martinis.

The tide was coming in.

A child pushed past me with two bags of cookies.

"Put them back," screeched the mother.

"But, Mom," the child whined.

"Fine. Fine. Keep one," said the mother, crumpled with annoyance. "But that's it. The other goes back. I mean it. And fast."

The checkout girl stared at the receipt tape, her fingers air-twirling her goofy bangs. She motioned over a manager and said lazily, "I don't know really how to do this. I mean I charged twenty-nine dollars instead of $2.90." The manager angled in next to her, glad to have something he could show the girl. "Like this," he said punching a flurry of numbers into the register.

I was never getting out of this store. I was going to be stranded on this side of the bridge with idiot families and morons who could not correctly punch in the price of potato chips. I considered junking the cart of food. But I wanted provisions. I wanted, even despite Pete, to not go home. I would figure something out about Pete. Maybe start a something if it would keep Paul happy at the beach for the fall. A dalliance would be fine, but I did not under any circumstance want some guy mooning about us.

I bagged my own five bags of groceries, the girl looking up from her register and saying, "Wow. Cool. That's a big help. Thanks."

The tide was in, water streaming over the road, which was still passable. I sped up to the house. But Pete's boat was not back. Finally I sighted the boat heading in. It still took almost an hour before they brought the boat in and the two of them got off, knocking against each other as they made their way up the beach. They looked as if they had been together, always.

"Hey, Sailorboy," I said, grabbing Paul into my lap. He squirmed off of me, standing up by Pete's leg.

"We saw you. We could see you for a long, long time," Paul said. "I caught four fish. What were they again, Pete? Two skate and what were the others?"

"Skate and whale," he said with a wink. "Hey, where's our chowder, Mom?"

Our chowder? Mom? Everything in me said get off this island. Where was I going? The island was my way to stay away from home.

"No. No. Mackerel, right, Pete?" Paul had not taken his eyes off Pete. I could feel the tilt of his swoon.

"Whatever you say, skipper," said Pete rubbing the top of my son's sweet wind-tangled head.

I could not bear that, the sight of Pete's fingers tousling Paul's hair. Or the way, the next day Paul kept running down to Pete's cottage to ask him one more question. After two more days and nights of my child cooing, "Pete thinks the blueberries are too sour this year and Pete thinks I will catch a bass next time fishing," I tight-lipped Pete's good-bye kiss and nodded blankly at Jeanette's, "Well, just say it and the shack's yours next summer," and took my boy away at top speed through a spray of incoming tidal water.

I took him back to our house where we shut and locked the door each night. Away away away from his boy crush.

Was it only a month later, sitting at dinner, when Paul said, "Miss Silken says we all have something valuable to say, that's why we are supposed to raise our hands," that I understood how wrong I had been? Pete was easy. Miss Silken was not after my attentions. It was Paul she wanted. I should have chosen a man's fingers in my boy's hair. I should have opened my mouth over his sandy mouth and stayed there where each day tides swept in and kept the rest of the world away.

What Is Going On in There?

I sit in my car, parked by the school fence, and wait for him. I wait all morning. I am afraid I will not be here on time when school lets out. I watch the school all morning for signs.

What is going on in there, inside the fence, inside the shut school doors? I see lights in the classroom windows, the ceiling rack of horrid fluorescent lights.

I see horrid turkeys pasted in windows, lopsided Pilgrim hats with their dark Pilgrim thanks.

I see Spot.

I want to climb the fence, come up to and knock softly on the window, say with the most spare and silent gestures that he must shush, not let on that I am there crouched just outside the window. It is the game. We are spies. He has infiltrated and been caught by the enemy. I am here now. I will get him out. It has been days, months, since his capture. He has undergone every sort of interrogation. Tortures have been carried out in the most routine of manners. He has done well. He has told nothing. He has been brave. I will rescue my boy.

Suddenly the playground is tilt full of children. They are everywhere in swarms. Not just one on a swing, but, somehow, three on each swing seat and one more pushing, twisting the chain so that all the children spin, arms, heads, legs flying, or they loft themselves off at the crest of the swing's rise and they are already running off, halfway up the monkey bars, crowding one another, pushing at one another. They are full tilt running at one another with hands and balls and fists and jump ropes and head-on crashings and jabs and fists and tagged running off and chasing and chasing balls and throwing balls, too hard they throw balls and at one another or just miss or a ball smacks in the surprised face of the drifting kid, or the ball intercepted and stolen off and then the chasing and the pouncing and the mad hard scrabble for the ball, and then the ball abandoned. Then there they go, the children up in all directions on the slide, piling on top of one another as they go down the slide and land in a heap of children off the slide while the ball rolls past them, unnoticed, rolling till it comes slower and slower to a stop.

I am up to the car window looking for my boy.

He is nowhere. He has not come out. All of my heart is at the window looking for Paul. But there are only other children, in jackets too big or squeezed into last year's toggle coat.

I try to breathe.

It is dizzying to watch their whirl and tag. They are in a skid.

"Me, me, me," they announce themselves. " I want the ball."

I am out of the car.When he was a baby, and I held him for hours on my legs looking at him, I wanted to memorize his body. Every mark, the five freckles on his forearm. I looked at the red birthmark on the inside of his leg. I knew already that I would need to find him. "I would know you by this."But there is no chance to check through the swirls of children, to find my one boy, with his odd marking, the snail of hair on his neck, the birthmark on the inside of his leg.

Near the fence, two boys conspire, lay out a game plan. They cannot stop moving. They have hours of the stillness of classrooms inside their small-boy bodies. How do they manage to stay still? How do these boys that even in sleep run through their beds, how do they sit still?

"Then we will get them and take them into our jail," says a boy with red hair. He has a stick that he pokes through the fence links.

"Where's jail?" asks the other, zippered into a ridiculous purple jacket.

"It's here! Idiot!" says Red Hair.

Red Hair and his cohort are off, and I watch as they rocket through the playground, hoping their mission leads him to me.

They blast through a knot of girls.

The girls do not even look up.

They circle back and blast again through girls who look now and yell and slap at the air after the boys zoom through. Red Hair, with his stick high and waving, is ready to poke out eyes.

Now I think I would not know Paul. He has been here among all these children, rubbing against these other children, so that he has erased anything that identifies him as my child. School has made of my child any child. He is like all the other children.

But there he is. There! Close to the fence. Running in a tight pack with three other boys. They turn and bank together, their bodies moving in a great joined tumble. They skim past the fence. His glance skims the fence but he does not see me. He sees only what is on his side, what is on the side of noise and skitter, where the children move together in a tussle.

I could touch him, call to him

The red-haired boy zooms up. He is alone, his friend lost somewhere on the playground. The red-haired boy wants trouble. He is on a mission for trouble, bumping into bodies to make his presence felt. He snaps his coat out, a whip that cracks through the air.

"Hey," shouts a boy. "That hurts!"

I press against the fence.

The red-haired boy pitches himself forward, ramming against a shoulder.

"Stop that!" I call. Not a child raises his head to my voice.

The red-haired boy is butting and ramming, through and back and into the pack of boys.

I am watching Paul who is not watching the red-haired boy. He is crouching with another boy, drawing with sticks in the mud. I move down the fence, closer to him. The two boys are bent over their work, their heads close, almost touching. They each have long sticks. They wield their sticks loosely, the sharp, forked ends poking near their faces. I see what will happen. The red-haired boy will hurl himself onto them. The sticks will poke out an eye, pierce a cheek, jab into the thin white skin at a collar.

But the red-haired boy flashes by them, chasing after a yelping boy.

They work, the boys leaning against each other for balance, drawing something according to a shared plan they devise in their quiet serious voices. I cannot make anything out.

"Look at what I can do," says Paul and he lifts his stick in the air and waves it in a wild loop.

"I can do that," says the other boy making his own looping gesture.

I am right next to him and he still does not see me.

"Let's trade sticks," says the boy.

"No," Paul says, "mine's better."

"I want that one," says the boy grabbing hold. They tug and tug. They are in a fist of grabbing, rolling atop of each other, the stick like a sharp line they are drawing.

"You get it, Loverboy," I shout before I have known I have shouted. "You get it. You get it."

He startles at my voice. His hands let go of the stick.

"I've got it," screams the other boy, rolling off and springing to his feet, the stick clutched to him.

Paul looks at me. Only for a second. *Go away.* That is what his quick look says. *Go away.*

Then he is off. He runs up to the boy and they both grab hold of the stick and ride it off away from the fence. I see them, with Paul steering them into the center of the playground, into the high cry of voices.

I stay at the fence.

He does not even once look back.

Primary Colors

"How is she this afternoon? Looks a little like she's coming around."

"If you call that coming around? Hypokinesia. To me she's a frozen statue with a few facial tics."

"Come on. Look, her eyes are open. That's a good sign. There's definitely increased motor function. What are her vitals?"

"I don't know. To me, she's still lost out there waiting."

"No, this lady's a fighter. She's on her way back."

Then, without wanting to, I became Mom, Mommy, even Mother.

"Mom," he said, stepping off the school bus. "Mom, I've got homework to do for school."

No more *Mama*, no invention of names, a *Miss My Darling* or *Lovely Mama* said in clever tones.

"I have things, not *I've got* things. Okay, Darling?" I tried to keep my voice even.

"But, Mom, I learned in school, you can say both. Both, Miss Silken says, are correct."

School was correct and I was suspect. It was that simple, as if suddenly he had to relearn the mix of colors and that all our work to find the vast array of greens was incorrect because there was a correct school method in which blue and yellow mixed simply made green. If I asked what he did in school, he hardly looked at me when he muttered, "Stuff."

Even later, all of the playground bathed from him, the tempera paints scrubbed from under his pared nails, even then, in the drowsy, night-lit dark of his room, it was, "Mother, I better go to sleep or I'll be sleepy in school."

Not a trace of her. Not a mention. Not a cozy lapsing moment where he snuggled in my arms before falling off to sleep with a tired, whispered, "Night, night, Miss My."

Miss My, she was gone. *Miss My Darling* disappeared, lost in a jiggle and taunt-ridden bus ride where he heard other boys say things about moms with unfair rules and table manners. For Loverboy it sounded exotic in its spongy normalcy. He began suggesting stricter rules, posting job charts, house chores, and he was, suddenly, counting food groups.

"Mom," he said, "it's not healthy to have cookies before supper."

Suddenly we were having *supper.* Not in my house. My house was not a supper house. It was not a house of paper napkins and grace. Mine was a house of milk in wineglasses, a strip of cherry licorice wrapped around a spoon.

Wednesday

"I have come for my son," I say at the Principal's office.

The secretary pricks up her head. "Whose mother are you?" she asks, looking at me with the skeptical look I think must be on her job description.

"I am here to pick up my son a little bit early from school," I say.

The secretary's desk is stacked high with files. I imagine that on each file a child's name is written on the tab and inside, the child is a series of scores and measures. Or worse, the children flattened and stuck inside the manila files.

"Yes, I understand," says the secretary, her voice unyielding. "But which child, exactly, is your son?"

I rummage: Cookie, Sweetiepie, Loverboy. It is taking too long. Concern flares across her face.

There is a boy sitting on the office bench, his feet not touching the floor. He has an ice pack jammed against his face.

"My son is Paul." I say in as even a voice as I can manage. There—I have said his name and, like a special code, the lock on her face relaxes. "Paul in Miss Silken's class, " I say. "I have to pick him up a bit early today."

"Yes, yes," says the secretary, nodding with each yes I take to mean the guard has let me in, but I am still under tight surveillance.

She glances at the clock, opens a large black book, flips through pages, looking back and forth from the book to the clock and back to the book. "There he is," she announces, "in art class." She shuts the book and puts it back in its same spot on her desk. She looks at me. I am supposed to say something. There is something that I must say to bring him here to me.

"Yes," I say, "I am afraid I have to take him out of art class to go to the doctor's."

I have said the magic word. Doctor. She smiles.

"I'll send for him then," she says importantly. I smile at her. She is glad not to be having a situation. I step back, trying to look like every mother who waits for her child. I am Paul's mother waiting to take Paul to the doctor's office.

"It will take a little time," she says. "You might have a seat."

I take a seat by the wall next to the boy pressing the ice pack up to his cheek. He looks at me from under his ice pack, waiting for me to talk to him, ready, I can see, to tell me all about it. I should say something, but I cannot think of anything motherly to say to the boy.

I think of the halls of the school, tiny corridors like veins. I try to feel where my boy is and pull him down the thin veins, bring him quickly here to me.

The secretary looks up, glancing at me from her desk. She is waiting for me, too. I am an unknown mother, a new mother, not a mother who has helped with school drives or classroom duties. Has she seen me yet on a class trip? Worse, I have interrupted the flow of the school day. I have made her open the black book of class schedules and give away information.

"Ouch," I say in a quiet, exaggerated voice, turning to the boy. "I hope at least you captured the bad guys."

"Nah, it's not too bad," says the boy eagerly. He lifts the ice off to reveal a red, frozen face, a bloody cut scorched down his cheek. "It doesn't even hurt."

I make myself smile.

"Well, you sure are a brave guy," I say.

The boy smiles. The secretary clucks her tongue. "With the scuffs this one gets in, it's a miracle he's got any face left on him at all."

We sit silenced on the bench, the boy and I, co-conspirators in this office, where both of us know questions can only get us in trouble.

"Hey," warns the secretary, "you get that ice pack back on your lucky face."

"But I don't need it. It doesn't even hurt."

"You better have it on your face when your mother walks in here. That's the second time this week you've dragged her down here."

I count one, two, three, four, five, six, seven, eight,

nine, ten, eleven, twelve, thirteen, fourteen, fifteen, right up to the moment I see him walk into the Principal's waiting room.

He is here. My son. I breathe.

"Hi," I say.

He looks right past me, over at the boy with the ice pack.

"Hey," he says eagerly, "what happened to you?"

"Paul," I say raising my voice to a pitch of importance, "we really don't have time."

He turns on me, fast, snarls, "What are you even doing here, Mom? Where are we going? School's not over. I want to stay at my school."

Spy Time

There is scratching behind the lawn chair and I drop the book I have not been reading. I squint against the sun so that it takes a moment to see the huge man coming at me, scraping a long stick, and then it takes a moment to make out that it is not a man.

"Lenny? What are you doing here?"

"Oh," he says leaning against the rake, "I'm sorry. I didn't mean to scare you."

I look at my watch. Ten in the morning.

"No school?"

Lenny shuffles, uncertain, as if speaking itself does not come naturally. He digs his boot under the small pile of leaves.

"I have a double study. Thought I better come over and get this done, you know, with school and stuff, it's hard to get over here."

There are so many hours in a day with a book I cannot read until I can even wait at the bus stop for Paul.

"I understand," I say.

"I'll come back or something if I'm bothering you or something." He says, turning to rake. There is a dark bruise just where his neck meets his T-shirt.

"What happened?" I ask and just as I ask I see it is not a bruise but some girl's mark. Lenny is not truly handsome but still the kind girls like, a messy, distracted countenance that far into his manhood will be mistaken for intensity. "Oh," I say smiling, "I see."

And, suddenly, Lenny is a little brazen, cocky, jutting his neck forward. "What can I say?" he says, leaning on the rake like a regular dandy.

It is almost too tempting. "You know, if you have a moment, can you come help me with something inside?" I would say. And then it might proceed, albeit predictably. Eagerness and instruction. The sheets speckled with leaf pieces. He would doze and wake, skipping the rest of his classes while I admired all the admirable earnest places on a teenage boy. Except I stay stuck in the lawn chair, the book closed in my lap, and watch Lenny rake. All there is are the too many hours in my day. All morning I watch, with such sadness, the ordinary grown boy my son had gone off to school to become.

Wednesday

"Don't tell me," says the secretary looking up. "It's already Wednesday?"

"Yes, it is Wednesday," I say, my face in its helpful P.T.A. smile.

"I'll send for him," she says and a fussy-looking girl appears from wherever in the Principal's office they store fussy good girls. There must be a closet filled with girls, girls so good, so eager to help that they are excused from class to run errands through the building, knocking—never too loudly—on classroom doors to deliver Xeroxes. These are the children who wheel overhead projectors through the school corridors, never speeding around corners, never cutting up in the hallways or needing a stern warning.

"Poor child," says the secretary. "How long will this go on for?"

"We are simply not sure, Mrs. Pomeroy," I say, adjusting my smile to a concerned narrow line. Now I call her by name. Mrs. Pomeroy. We chat. I am known to her—the Wednesday mom who brings her son, Paul, to the doctor.

But, of course there is no doctor. I have invented a schedule of shots at the allergist's. I take him out early every Wednesday. I take him out, I have told Mrs. Pomeroy, a little extra early so that I can get a bit of lunch into him before the shots.

"He tends to be exhausted after the shots," I say, "and I try to get something healthy in his stomach."

The allergist, I have told Mrs. Pomeroy, is worried that Paul is even allergic to air.

She winces. "That poor child," she says. "We've had so many children suffer with allergies. I remember there was another boy in the school who it turned out was allergic to the metal on the cafeteria silverware. Can you imagine? The mother spent all year running him to doctors, not to mention the crazy fortune she must have spent, before they located what it was that was making the boy puff up. And you can't believe, you just could never even imagine that face. His face about doubled in size."

"Oh," I say, a seen-it-all-in-waiting-rooms look on my face, "you would not believe what an allergic response can be."

"Really?" she says. She is waiting, her plucked-to-a-question eyebrows pulled even higher. I see how it will be. Wednesday after Wednesday, feeding her little horror stories, children with lips the size of watermelons, fingers that swell to the point of fingernails popping off, the children who need so much medication they lose their memory and walk out into waiting rooms unsure of which parent is their mother. I will keep her stuffed and drugged on medical wonders and nightmares, the promise of technologies. The children who cannot breathe air or drink water. The children who must exist on black bars of nourishment prescribed in replacement of all foods.

"Really?" she says again, waiting for a horror to inform her day.

"There is a girl," I tell her, "we see her every week. Her skin is so raw, so thinned with some crazy, rare reaction that she cannot bear the pressure of clothes. Her own clothes hurt her. Her parents make her gowns of silk. And still her skin bleeds and stains the silk."

Mrs. Pomeroy's face folds into itself, horrified and excited.

It is impressive, really, how remarkably flawless I have become at these inventions.

I am ready to go on, to create the delicious agony of this girl's existence for the starved Mrs. Pomeroy. But here is the door with the good girl and behind her Paul dragging his jacket.

I am at the door before Paul can come into the office.

I am quick, efficient, no time for talk.

No time for Mrs. Pomeroy's questions.

"Hi Paul," I say in my composed Wednesday voice. "We must hurry up, Paul, or we shall be late."

Use It

"You gave me the name," he snapped at me one night at dinner. "Why can't you just use it, Mom?"

I only wanted what I have always wanted. *Loverboy* and *Miss My Darling*. The two of us in our bedecked world, listening to Beethoven's Seventh, following the evolving, reinvented refrain. The two of us not as members of that other shabby world but in small forays going off to view it, to examine it, looking over it as gods coming down to check on the shackled, tawdry habits of man.

Marty says to Sybil as they clutch each other on the sofa, "I would do anything for you, my sweetness." I tried other names. I called him *honey* and *sweetie* and *honeybear* and *sweetheart* and *sweetbear*.

I said, "Mr. Darling, will that be a glass of apple or orange juice?

"Hey, Cookie, want a cookie?"

I said, "Wake up, Sunnyboy."

"Mom," he said flat and resolute, "my name is Paul."

Boxcar

"Mother," he says, "can we get out of here?"

He looks pleasingly small in the freight yard; the cars form a steep wall, suddenly shifting from one track to the next as they fan out, rolled from the hump. There are loud diesel engines stalled but still left running, though no one working the trains is in sight. Everything is large—large sound and the large moving heft of freights backing up, stopping, uncoupled, then a grinding forward of gears. A Union Pacific car bangs, crashing against an Erie car and they lock, coupled.

I lead us over to a boxcar, its wide door slid open. I lever up with a twist until I sit in the boxcar's open mouth.

"Give me your arms," I reach down.

He holds up his arms and I try lifting, but he dangles and my hold is not firm. "Do over," I say dropping him. "You have to help a little. Jump."

It is bigger than I imagined from the outside. We keep to the walls, our feet slapping loudly on the boards.

On the walls a scrawl of unreadable words. In a careful cursive: *I am Betty in Minneapolis on Christmas Eve. God Bless. Who are you?*

"Are we ready to ride hobo?" I ask, ready to play.

"Sure," he says. "Where are we going?"

"Well, we are coming up from Texas on the Santa Fe line." I crouch, campfire style, and Paul crouches beside me, both warming our hands over our play scrap fire. "We are hungry, crazy hungry. Not a morsel for two days."

"But we go on to Colorado and we eat a buffalo," he says, rubbing his belly. "Then what happens?"

"A scuffle, nothing too serious, outside of Durango, but it turns out friendly and we join up with Extravaganza and Uncle Pierre, who are out to find their fortune, which they suppose is a game of hearts they heard about in the Windy City. But we keep riding the rails. Where do we go next?" I ask, ready for him to take a turn.

"Mother," he says, suddenly standing giving a yank by the wrist. "Come on. What are we doing here?"

"We are here on our way to a rendezvous with an Indian chief in Cheyenne," I say, trying to keep him with me in our story.

Then he is at the door of the boxcar, slithering on his belly, until he drops off, feet first. He might keep going, walking out the gates of the freight yard, up to the unfamiliar city streets, down some street and into another life. But he stops at a distance from me, and shouts, "Hello Mom! Hello Mom! I thought you were supposed to take me to a doctor!"

Anywhere, Now, Anywhere

Here is the week. I wait for Wednesday. Then it is Wednesday and all morning I rush, preparing an elaborate lunch packed in many containers in a straw basket. I drive to the school to take us away from school. I park the car in an open lot. We eat a cold soup and a rice dish, olives and cucumbers and a pie with fresh whipped cream. He barely touches the food. Then I take us walking. I point at funny signs, make small talk. He feels unfamiliar.

"Will I get back for dismissal?" he says.

"Not today," I say.

"How long?" he asks.

"How long what?" I ask.

"Will we wait?"

"Walk faster," I say.

"We're late?" he says.

"No," I say.

"If we're not late, then what are we?" he says.

"Walking," I say.

"Where?" he says.

"A Roam About, remember them?" I say.

"The doctor. I thought we were going to the doctor's."

"Well, we are not," I say.

"I want to go to back to school."

"Forget it," I say.

Paul stops. "Well, I have to go to school. It's the law."

I look him back trying to match his scowl. "I hate the law and I hate your school."

"Oh, Mom," he says, looking at me with such stern pity. "My teacher says that hate is a very bad word and no one should ever ever ever say it."

I walk fast and hear him follow.

I walk to a highway overpass. The metal fence has a bend and I lean into it. The highway below vibrates in my feet. It is speed underneath, cars, cars, their dizzying speed. I let my eyes shut, hear the hum of cars, their going. Paul is there; he tugs then holds onto my coat, his body tightening against my side.

It would do well to find a passion.

He is not looking at the highway but up at me. I close my arm around him, bending so that our heads are at the same height.

"We are fine," I say, my cheek against his. "Close your eyes and listen. We can go anywhere, now, anywhere in the whole world."

Wednesday

In comes the doctor. Today, I am honored. I believe it is Dr. Spock himself. He huddles in consultation. They discuss residual effects, the neuropsychological sequelae, apraxia, echolalia. No doubt the Good Doctor himself has consoling words for a suffering parent. But the Good Doctor speaks firmly, with furrowed brow and finger wagging. Look at his mouth move, the fleshy bottom lip, chewing up and down while he reminds me that every child will, despite the secret wishes of every parent, not remain a baby. "Look, Look, Look. Adorable!" exclaims Dr. Spock. The baby insists on feeding himself, his dear, chubby fingers smooshing pureed carrots on his cheeks. A child wants, needs, will inevitably branch into the world. The child must master these lessons.

Listen, dear Dr. Spock, I read the books. Every one of them. Then I threw the books out.

"Wednesday?" Mrs. Pomeroy laughs. "Come on, this time even I know it's Tuesday."

"Oh, is it?" I joke, light, a regular-school-mom laugh. Now I am known. A mom about the school, a concerned mom, an active mom, not one of the moms who calls in messages, a mom never seen except at class conferences. I laugh with the school secretary.

Then I turn on her. Controlled, serious. "No, something has come up and we need to get Paul to the doctor again today."

"Is it serious?" she asks, ready for a diversion.

But today I have no chatter, though it is clear there will be a required bit of chatter.

"The doctor said," I say, "he thinks this is the only week he will need to come in twice—but he is not making any promises."

"Isn't he all right?" she asks. "I thought he was doing so much better."

I go the route of the I-am-not-going-to-be-an-alarmist mom. The mom who lets you know it is serious, really serious, by just how little she is really willing to say.

"I think it will be fine," I say, sitting down on the waiting bench.

"I'll send for him," she says, suddenly serious and eager to do her job efficiently and with a schoolworthy, secretarial respect for privacy.

I am silent. I sit on the bench, waiting, while she checks the schedule book, and sends another mysteriously appearing good girl down for him.

Mrs. Pomeroy goes about trying to look as if she is

working, a file drawer opened, shut, reopened, envelopes slit.

I try to concentrate on my plan to give him a day he cannot refuse. I woke to the thrill of an idea, something that would bring him back to me—since he wants the normal, I will give him a typical boy's adventure. Nothing fancy. Something for regular boys, a trip to the toy store. Then ice cream. Perhaps a visit to a fun art gallery where the artist has built an entire city out of sugar cubes, a city with a shaking sugar subway and even a sweet city jail. No van Goghs for us today. We will sit on the sugar-cube subway and scan the map of the invented city's underground system. Or if the gallery is too strange, maybe we will eat a second ice cream. We will not stay out too late, just late enough for a movie. He will grow sleepy and will crawl up in my lap in the theater, fitting himself comfortably in my arms. He will nap and wake at the end of the movie. He will hold my hand and shuffle back to our car, drifting back to sleep while I drive us home. I will pull into the garage and carry him inside, cradling the sleeping weight of his body up to his room, undressing him down to his T-shirt and giving him a little kiss good night.

"This must be so hard on you," she says, finally unable not to speak.

"It is hard," I say, looking up to meet her stare for the briefest moment.

"I just can't imagine," she says.

"Me neither," I say.

I hear, at last, steps in the hall. The clipped-heel steps of his prissy escort. And Paul's scuffing feet coming toward me. They are quick, eager-sounding steps.

But it is not Paul and the girl who come in through the door. Instead, Miss Silken walks in and stands in front of me. Where, I wonder, did she dream up that name Miss Silken—soft and serious? And how is it she manages to dress in her blouses and skirts and dressy shoes in a classroom of paint and paste and sneezy kids?

"I need a moment to speak with you," says Miss Silken. She is tense and her words have the sound of attempted confidence.

"Well, yes, surely," I say standing up. "But I am afraid it will have to wait. We are in quite a hurry today. A terrible hurry, actually. Maybe we can speak tonight?"

"I think we need to speak now," she says.

"That is impossible right now," I say. "I need to take Paul. Is he on his way?"

"He won't come in. He refuses. He's outside the office," says Miss Silken.

I laugh. The laugh sounding, surprisingly, just as relaxed as I need it to. "I do not blame him," I say.

"We need to talk," repeats Miss Silken. She moves her hands like a little woman, almost a child herself if she were not dressed in a blue silk blouse and a straight skirt. She is not budging.

"Certainly," I lie, "we need to work together to make this easy for Paul. But I am afraid that today we really are late."

"He says there's no doctor," says Miss Silken in a slow, dropped voice.

I get louder, joke, "A child's imagination is a mighty beast," I smile. Over Miss Silken's blond head, I see Mrs. Pomeroy's face frozen into a squeal of horror.

"He's been very upset for a while. He swears to me there is no doctor," she says. She lifts and drops her shoulders. "I didn't take him seriously, at first," her hands twitter, embarrassed.

I look right at her. "What are you saying, Miss Silken?"

"I'm not saying anything but what Paul has said to me. That there is no doctor. He has explained to me that you just take him places." She forces herself to look up at me, "Maybe you could bring in a note, something officially from his doctor?"

"Excuse me," I say. "If there is a problem and, obviously, my son is having a problem, I do not really think that you are doing a very professional job coming down here with some crazy rigmarole. But right now I need my son or we will be late."

Then, with a brush, I am past Miss Silken in her fancy blue blouse, out of the office and into the hallway. I see Paul hunched close to the wall, under a reef of sea-creature collages. My hand is on Paul and I am saying as I push him through the school doors, "You do not look right. I called Dr. Spigman this morning and he said that after last night's bout to come to the office right away."

He Is Ours

What I did not expect was her positively enthusiastic tone. The Principal saying, "I'm so sorry for your discomfort yesterday. Let's all get together and try to work out a comfortable situation for everyone."

"Yes," I say, attempting a reasonable pitch, "that would certainly be good."

"I'm so glad you feel that way. Friday? Noon? Would that work for you?"

"Noon is great," I say in the most obnoxiously cheerful voice I can muster. "That will give me the morning to finish some work that is under a critical deadline."

"We look forward to meeting with you," the Principal says, adding, "Paul is a good child. He is settling into his first year of school with wonderful ease. He has none of the shyness you might see in a child entering a room where the other children were all together in kindergarten. We all just love his enthusiasm."

I hear the message through her upbeat nonsense.

Loud and clear she is talking to me. Lady, she is saying to me, lady, he may have been late getting to us, but now he is ours.

They make me wait. I sit on my same Wednesday bench. Mrs. Pomeroy is insistently busy, shuffling through a fan of folders, doing everything she can possibly do not to look over at me. She has been called in and taken to task for having cavorted with me. Why was no one alerted? They have interrogated her. Is it not her task to notice anything suspicious? "But," she draws her lips tightly, "how could I have possibly known?" She tells them about the girl with the gossamer silk gowns. I wonder which makes her more distraught—that she has been called in or that the atrocities I described are not as horribly real as she has enjoyed them to be.

She cannot bear it and she looks over. I think she will speak, but she does not say anything except for taking deep, snorting sighs. Her phone rings and she snaps it up, clutching it to her ear.

"Yes," she says quietly.

She looks over at me. I smile at her.

"Yes, yes," she says swiveling in her chair so that she sits profile to me. "Yes, she is."

Then with an effort that is ridiculous, she turns her head back to me and says in a studied voice, "They'll be ready for you in a few minutes."

"Whatever you feel, you really are not alone," the Principal smiles at me. She holds her coffee at her lips.

Steam rises and she blows dragon-like as she speaks. "So many mothers have such a terrible time of it these first months of school. It's rough but I'll admit, thank God for a little empty-nest anxiety or I wouldn't have any of those hard-working moms on my P.T.A." She sips her coffee and laughs a little laugh.

I laugh. This is my job: to reassure everyone that I am not what they think I am. I make a point of looking at the Principal and at Miss Silken who sits posture-perfect in her chair. Miss Silken regards me quietly. She looks back and forth between the Principal and me. The chairs have been arranged in a loose triangle, the Principal's chair moved out from behind her big gray desk. I am being told by this arrangement that we are all equals in finding a solution. This meeting has been carefully orchestrated and the young and lovely Miss Silken is eager to show the Principal how professional a teacher she can be.

"I've considered a parent-buddy system," the Principal says to me in a confidential tone as if she were sharing a clever idea she has wanted to share with someone for a long time. "I mean, think of it, we pair up the children to walk in the corridors or at assembly. The first week of school we buddy fifth graders with kindergartners so that the little ones should each have a big kid to look after them. The children love it. The little ones feeling safe and also known by our older students. And the fifth graders, you'd be surprised, they take the job very seriously. Well, why not old and new moms? It's a huge transition for everyone."

She smiles, bubbling over with the momentous idea she has just expressed. "It is an intriguing idea, right?"

"Sure," I parrot, "intriguing."

"Maybe you'll help me. You are not working, are you?" she asks. They have been trying to make some sense of my situation. Too many blanks that must be filled in. The father question will be asked in due time.

"Yes, actually—" I stall, deciding what job will intimidate them most. "I run a cell lab. Fluorescence research, primarily. " I have to force myself to look at the Principal because I want too much to see my effect on the tiny Miss Silken, who has wrapped my son around her tiny polished fingers, the woman he looks at every day with rapt attention.

"Really?" she says, definitely unprepared. "I had no idea. You are a scientist? How interesting. Someday I hope you will explain the nature of the research exactly. Fascinating."

I nod, making sure not to show too much delight.

"That must be tough," the Principal continues, working to get back to her agenda. "A single working mom. I don't know how you do it. I hope there's a dad somewhere close by to give you a break every once in a while."

I have practiced in advance, prepared to say that Paul has a concerned and active father, but I let myself take a peek at Miss Silken. Her legs cross at the ankles, like some good behavior she is trying to model, and her head, too, has that good-behavior tilt that says, See? I am doing a good job of listening. It is a look I have newly seen on Paul.

I snap, "I am not looking for breaks from my child."

The Principal's eyes go fuzzy with empathy. I have made a mistake, opened the door, and here it comes.

"It's been rough, hasn't it?" says the Principal. "Well, there's nothing wrong with that," she continues. "You feel far away from your son. That's natural. We can help you today by letting you know a little more about Paul's life in school. You can only imagine how many parents call saying that, according to their child, nothing happens in school all day. Except snack and maybe recess. Maybe Miss Silken, his teacher, can tell you just how Paul is doing in these first months of joining our first-grade community."

Miss Silken perks her little body up even higher in her chair. She can barely contain her alert, careful self.

"He's adjusting very well to the classroom expectations, " she starts. Her voice sweetly bubbles over each word. How have I let my son spend a day in the room with a woman who speaks as if she is trying to be a doll?

"Paul, he's always the first to hang up his jacket and start right in on an appropriate activity. He likes work in the block area or even the writer's notebook. He is attentive and social, and seems eager to make friends with the other children in the room."

Miss Silken looks over at the Principal. The Principal smiles. I am supposed to say something but I am not sure what I am supposed to say.

"Yes," I say, fixing a smile on my face, softening my voice to reassure them. "Paul has mentioned building with blocks."

"He's a great boy. But I have to say that sometimes," Miss Silken looks down at her hands, "he's a bit formal. His speech, for example. And I sense a bit of nervousness in Paul."

"Quite normal," interrupts the Principal. "He's after all having his first schooling experience, isn't he?"

I think of our snowed-in afternoons, books in towering piles next to the sofa, big bowls of soups, making up names for the strange unnameable vegetables, and the waitress carefully trying to get us to form our lips to pronounce the Greek or Vietnamese or Hebrew phrases.

"Yes, normal, but his anxiety seems a bit more extreme than that of the other children," Miss Silken says in her lilting professional voice.

"Excuse me, Miss Silken. Do you understand Paul's exceptional capacities?" I stare down at her until I make her shift and fidget in her chair.

"All my children are special," she says, looking over at the Principal.

"No, he is not just any child. Have you even noticed that he is way above all the other children? Have you even noticed that his intelligence is remarkable or that his creativity is utterly breathtaking?"

"Actually," Miss Silken pipes in, "Paul's really comfortably situated in the classroom. He's a hard worker and that helps him keep up with some of the stronger children."

"How old are you?" I ask.

She fidgets, "Excuse me?"

"How old are you, Miss Silken?"

"Twenty-six," she says, sounding uncertain, as if she is working diligently on the calculation.

"You do not have children?"

She smiles her little doll smile. "No kids of my own. But my students almost feel like my own kids. Really."

"My son is not your kid," I snap. I should stop. Make nice to the good teacher. But, suddenly, I am having the first real fun I have had since Paul has left me for this miserable school with this little doll of a teacher who has probably never listened to Stravinsky's *Sacre du Printemps*. I am getting ready to say that I do not want her mild pedestrian ideas infecting my son.

"One moment. Please," says the Principal, putting down the cup. She leans over her legs, her hands planted on her knees. "This is not constructive. And what we all need to remember is Paul. We want to help this transition go as smoothly for Paul as possible. We need to work as a team. Taking him from school is confusing to him while he is working so hard to learn the complicated routines and expectations of his teachers. It's disruptive. However good your intentions, you must understand it is disruptive."

I look at Miss Silken and the Principal. Nothing I can think of to say is sayable. They are waiting for my reassurance, my promise to cut the antics. They will allow me to help around school if I behave. Maybe come in for a science assembly. Explain cell fluorescence. Or, better yet, just disappear and leave them alone with their smooth-running programs, their curriculum plans and measured-learning increments.

"But his doctor says," I say.

"No doctor," says the Principal with a flip of her hand. "There is no doctor."

"I can bring in whatever medical documents you need to see." I muster. "You must understand," I start to say and then, suddenly, I see how it does not matter what I say. This is merely a courtesy gesture.

I stand. "Miss Silken," I address her directly, "perhaps in your extensive studies, you have heard of the educator Maria Montessori. It was she who described the conventional classroom as a place, and I believe I can quote her now, where children are 'like butterflies mounted on pins, one fastened each to his place.'"

Miss Silken's nose wrinkles. She has a mission—every teacher loves a mission—to protect her student from his sick mother. Now I understand that I have been the subject of special meetings. Records are kept. Perhaps a professional has already observed Paul. They have got my son. *Lady, he is ours.* Paul and Miss Silken have had special chats. She has tapped him on the shoulder when the lines were forming for recess. "Let's talk," she has said, her hand resting on his little shoulder. "You can trust me," she has cooed. She has told him that she is on his side. "Children don't lie," she says to him one afternoon while the other children have gone off to music. They sit in little chairs at a round table, Miss

Silken almost as small as Paul. "Draw a picture," she encourages him. "Yes, I care about you, so much."

I have to get out of the room. The Principal stands and Miss Silken jumps up, too.

"Please sit," the Principal says.

"Surely, if not Montessori, both of you must have at least heard of Emerson, Ralph Waldo Emerson. Emerson is, for all intents and purposes, Paul's father. Emerson says, 'You will always find those who think they know your duty better than you know it.'"

"Please," the Principal says, walking close. "We must remain the adults and consider Paul."

"No," I hiss. "Emerson says, 'That which each can do best, none but his Maker can teach him.' Oh, I see you do not understand my point. Let me try to approach this using your rather more primitive language. I absolutely do not and will never *consider* my son *with* anyone else."

When I walk out past Mrs. Pomeroy clutching the schedule book, I think, Lady, go on and try to follow him all day in your Big Schedule Book. Take a good look at your schedule, Mrs. Pomeroy. Tilt your eager blond head, Miss Silken. But he is not yours for the having, ladies.

Then, opening the office door I hear something like a wave, the rustle of silk, and, as though no time at all has passed, I think, "Oh, it is Mrs. Yarkin." I am giddy. I am no longer at that other door, ringing, waiting for Mrs. Yarkin. She is here waiting, ready to guide me to where I can safely take my son.

Do You Hear Me?

Do you hear me behind you, Emerson?

On the path through the lower meadow, the grass grown waist-high and black-eyed Susans in delinquent patches along the path, the bright hooray of daylilies. Ahead you look like a boy with his father's big shovel, dragging it behind you, as it bumps over rocks, the metal blade bouncing and wobbling over the rutted path. I am following you, stopping behind you when you stop to hoist the shovel over your shoulder but you are tired and hardly even get it to your shoulder before you let it slip down and it drags again behind you.

You stop to inspect the Queen Anne's lace. You cannot stop your inspecting, can you? The tight knotted skein, the open round collars with their center drops of dark red. Yes, Emerson, like dried blood.

You are in a hurry but you are in no rush.

How will you dig deeply enough? I will come forward to help. Good. That is good. I think I know what I am looking for.

All Fixed Up

Most everything in the end we do not need.

Pack a box for him. Pack a box for me. Round up a box of those essential books we must always have near to us. I sort through his drawings, but choose, in the end, to roll them all up to bring along. I stack his shoe-box museums and our collection of bright pottery shards from the backyard excavation. Leaving is as simple as leaving a rental room. This part is quick. And then the rest is tidying up, leaving things in their proper condition. Everything must be cleaned, the rooms straightened up, our beds left made. A final sweep of the bathrooms, wiping down the sink, pulling our hair in thready clumps from the drains. A vacuum of each room we have lived in.

Then down to the garage to pack the car. Everything fits. I even decorate, taping one of his pictures to the visor.

With everything fitted into the car, I have time,

finally, to set this squall of a garage in order. The garage had always been our one unkept place, half-rigged shelves weighed down with what did not fit neatly inside our house. It was a place full of the mixed-around smells of oil and rust, a rubber smell that made me itchy.

Out with the half-filled gallon cans, their collars of dried, rubbery paint-sealing lids. Out with open Ball jars of ten-pound nails, jars of assorted screws and washers and stoppers. Out with knotted string, the snapped balsam dowels, our years of busted kites. But now it will be clean. They will be ordered shelves. It will be ready when we are ready to leave. No more musty garage with its junked heap of tricycles and fire trucks, the dusty torn beach umbrellas. I even bring down the vacuum, bring the long hose down here to the garage where it sucks up dust from corners, sucks up dust from where it is sheeted against the leaning sled. I leave the vacuum down here, where it can stay for our trip. *She put him in the bathtub to see if he could swim. He drank up all the water. He ate up all the soap. He tried to eat the bathtub, but it wouldn't go down his throat.* I never wanted a husband and I never wanted a home. Now all is fixed up, ready for leaving. We are going.

Where Are We Going?

He says, "Where are we going?"

We are strapped in, seat belts buckled. He looks so small in the driver's seat. His hands are on the steering wheel, frisking all over it, all at once.

"The first thing is position," I say from the passenger seat. "Put your hands at ten minutes to one o'clock."

"Stop joking, Mom," he says, casting a funny look over at me. "I can't drive."

"This is the ignition." I reach over and start to push the key into the ignition.

"Let me do that! I want to do that," he says, grabbing my hand.

"Fine, give it a try." He looks at me, his face twisted in a question. He takes the key out of my hand and starts jabbing at the ignition.

"Fit it. It is like a puzzle." He turns the key, poking until it threads into the ignition.

"Turn it to the right," I say, showing with my hand a right-hand turn. I love his quiet concentration as he practices turning the steering wheel. I reach my leg across for the gas pedal, straining until, with barely a toe, I push it and the engine turns over a little chokey and the car is on.

"The car's on!" He startles. He had been expecting play.

"That is right."

"I can't drive." He looks at me with all the distrust of a schoolboy.

"I know, Paul. This is a lesson."

"But the car is on."

"Yes."

"Where are we going?" It is the same horrible, distrusting question from days when I take him out of school.

"Oh, Paul," I say with the flip authority of a teacher, "we are not going anywhere. You have a lot to learn before we can leave this garage."

"Okay, what do I do? How do I do it?"

"Try your hands at ten to one. Almost. Close. Good."

Even cleaned, it is hard to stay in the garage. I want to go back inside with my cozy boy, cuddle in a chair, and read a storybook. But inside he said, "Call me Paul." There is no going back inside.

"Left-hand turn," I call out, and he puts on the left-turn signal, checks the rearview mirror and the side-view mirror, says, "I'm turning," turning the wheel, the right hand crossing over the left in a smooth arc, completing the circle. He makes a slight jag to straighten the wheel.

"You are going to be a good good driver."

"I am?"

"Yes, Sweetie. Yes, you are."

"I want to go inside," he says abruptly, letting go of the wheel.

"We cannot go inside, Paul. We have not done the course." I have said something wrong. *Sweetie.* He can be with me only if I remain the teacher.

"What course?"

"Please concentrate. Think about your hands and what I say."

I say we are on a long straight two-lane road. There is a left-hand turn to take on Dream Road. Dream Road is a winding road, plenty of strange things on that road. Look! Does he see the licorice trees with their candy leaves? He better swerve away from the fallen tree and there up ahead—are those pink cows out grazing in the middle of the lane? Gracious, look! Here is a car driving backward. Be careful. Now off this road and on to Easy Street. Well, is it, after all, so easy, Easy Street? What is that waterfall doing rushing over the road, and gold is great and everything, but are piles of it really necessary right in the middle of the road? We drive on, as I talk the journey and he steers us through near and certain disasters.

I tell him what is ahead. Dinosaurs grazing dangerously close to the road. Parakeets playing swoop and tag. Drivers driving with scarves around their faces. He must listen to me carefully or our car is bound to get hit.

He takes a hand off the wheel and starts some fooling about with his tooth.

"Two hands on the wheel," I caution. "Are you watching the road?"

"You always drive with one hand," he pouts, not letting go of the tooth. I hear the thready, wet twisting as he plays with the tooth.

"Hey, do you want to learn to drive or what?"

"No, I want to go inside. I know how to drive already." He is working hard at the tooth.

"So, you want it out?" I will do anything to have him back, to keep him with me.

"Uh huh," he muffles, his fingers still in his mouth.

"Let me yank it."

"What? You will?"

"Sure," I say in an easy voice. "But then we must stay here."

"Here?" he says sleepily.

"Yes, we are sleeping in the car."

"Why?"

"So the fairy finds us."

"No, Mom, you need to put it under your pillow."

"No, Paul, you must sleep on the spot where the tooth fell out."

"That's not right," he says adamantly.

"Yes, Paul. Which of us has lost her teeth? Which of us has received her tooth-fairy visits?"

I hear his silent evaluation, his careful figuring his way through this.

Outside the window the car light shines on the cleaned-up metal shelves. The car engine runs. The vacuum cleaner is in its place, the nozzle jammed into its place in the exhaust pipe, the hose fitted tightly through the back car window.

"Fine," he says grumpily. "Fine."

I unstrap myself and then Loverboy. I am tired, dizzy. He yawns, leans in a heap himself against me.

"So do it," he says suddenly sounding wakeful, bossy.

I reach into his opened mouth. "Wider, Mister."

He starts to say something but my fingers are already inside his mouth where I finger the loosened tooth. It comes out easily. He could have gotten it himself, I think, with a twist or two more. But the little chiclet tooth in my fingers is tiny, so tiny I think I could lose it there in his mouth and we might not find it even in his little mouth.

"Here," I say. "Is that what you want?" I try to taste the air for what I know is tasteless.

"Let me have it. Let me have it."

It is hard not to take in his pleasure, there is such force behind it. But that is all forward force. To the next and the next tooth, toward the next grade and third grade and the school dance and past to late nights out with friends who barely have the manners to mutter a hello to me as I sit in the worn-down house with my mounting pile of books. His pleasure is the pleasure of every graduation, until I will hardly remember the brief years when he was a boy I called Loverboy.

I am right. I am saving my son from the ordinary. I am saving him from an obvious life.

Loverboy is still my exceptional child. The child of such careful making. He is the passion Marty and Sybil said would make me happy. I was happy. And yet there will be a parade of school picnics, check marks, myriad days with tiny ordinary successes or failures. In a few years he will be no different than any other boy, like a yard kid come to earn pocket money to show off to girls. He would have been just another good kid. A Lenny.

Already, I can barely make him out from the next child.

Who is the mother that does not want to keep her child from the ruin of the normal? I do not understand.

I take his hand and put the tooth in it. "Careful," I warn, "do not drop it."

"How much will she give me?"

"Who?"

"The tooth fairy, Mom. Where do I put it? Are you sure she's going to find it? What if she doesn't? Why would she look in the car?"

I take off my light jacket. "Put it here. In the pocket. We shall use the jacket as your pillow. Fairies go for whatever is under your head." We wipe the tooth and drop it in the jacket pocket. There is a little button and it comforts him, closing the pocket flap, securing it with a button.

I fold the jacket, arrange it behind his head. He lets me do these things. I reach across him, pull the seat lever, lowering it.

"There," I say. "She will find you as soon as we are both asleep."

"You are going to sleep, too?"

"Yes, sir, Paul. I want to stay right beside you."

"Good," he says.

"Really? You mean that?"

"Yes, Mom," he says, his voice thickening with sleep. The gentleness of his voice wants to make me carry him inside.

I snap on the car lights to look at him. What mother does not love the child's face on its way to sleep, the way it falls back to the face of the baby, even the sucking at the mouth, like the child's residual dream of working securely at the mother's breast?

Has a mother ever loved a child more?

I swallow all the white pills I have brought to keep me with him, right next to him. I breathe and try to feel the gas entering me, already blocking the oxygen in my blood.

I want to wait until he is deeply asleep to lift his head and remove the tooth from the pocket and slip in a dollar. I do not want to disturb him. In the morning it will be just us two without the others.

We shall wake in our own world.

It will be only our bright morning.

And we can celebrate Loverboy with his first tooth dollar.

I take his still chubby hand in my hand and wait.

I am dizzy.

Then the silent fumes and the sour pills work their magic and I do not have the chance to give him his dollar.

But it is good just to wait in the dark holding hands.

Loverboy and Miss My Darling.

For forever.

Like that, we go to sleep.

And like that, we are gone.

Vitals

"She's awake. Did she just wake?"

"Oh no, she came to pretty much last night. Turned the corner last night. Check the charts. Heart and sed rate are fine. She's breathing on her own. Even talking quite a bit."

"Well, that's a turn."

"We sure have ourselves a live girl now. A regular Chatty Cathy. Coherent, too. Everything about the child. Paul this and Paul that."

"I suppose soon we'll have heard more than we want."

"I'll tell you, you can't be rid of her. I go off my shift and she's on every corner. Cover of the paper. The two of them, her and the poor boy. People all putting in their two cents about what was going on. Like no one has ever done anything to a kid before."

"What do you think was going on?"

"Oh, please. Don't ask. I'm taking care of her but I can't bear to think of the poor kid."

"You see the news? The newspapers? They're having a field day. Headlines like Tooth-Fairy Magic Saves Child."

"That's a new one. I saw one about a neighbor, some kid who came by supposedly to do a lawn job, opened the garage to get a rake, and found them both in the car."

"No, now they say the child got out of the car to go up to his room and put his tooth under his pillow. Seems he only got partly inside the house before he collapsed. But that was all it took to save his life."

"Imagine, a tooth! That's as close to magic as I've heard in a long time. That is, if he lives."

"Well, I heard downstairs that he was already released."

"But I'd heard he was dead, more or less."

"They said it was that close. Thought he wouldn't come around. About as badly poisoned as she was. But that's Pediatrics for you. I worked down in Pediatrics I.C.U. my first year. What would take an adult eight weeks, takes a kid three or four days. Once he came out of the coma, they say he bounced back and was up and playing. Nurses say he's a charmer. A lovely boy, manners and smart like you wouldn't believe."

"Miracle, really, either of them lived."

"Nurses say first thing he did was ask for his mom. Started crying. Wanted to come up and give her a kiss. Said she'd get better right away if he kissed her. Breaks your heart, they say, the way the boy loves the mother. Even tried to sneak up and get in here. Breaks your heart. And there isn't going to be any hiding from him what she did."

"Oh, I expect it will be the whole deal. There'll be a trial and everyone will get up with some foolishness to report. And the kid? He'll be snapped up by Child Services, spend years going through fosters."

"I'm not so sure about all that. People coming out from who knows where, coming out of the woodwork, saying they're the boy's relations. Already there are even two men claiming to be the father. Two men! And from two totally different cities. That's a fine one."

"Look at her. Hard to think what could make her do it. If you want to kill yourself, kill yourself. But then why have a kid in the first place?"

"Do you have any?"

"No, dear. I know myself a bit. Couldn't stand them hanging on me every second."

"Please. I have three myself. Still don't know how we do it some days. Glad just to get everyone tucked in by the end of the day. But by morning I'm glad to see them again. Love them with all my heart."

"What about her? Think she did?"

"What?"

"Love the boy?"

"Who knows? I expect most mothers do, in their own way, love their kids. But you never can tell."

"Maybe she just couldn't take it, all alone with a kid all the time. Having to take care of a kid all alone."

"Well, she took care of that. She made sure, didn't she? If that's all she wanted, if all she wanted was to get out of taking care of her child, then she made pretty certain the child was never going to spend a single day with his mother ever again."

Victoria Redel has published a book of short fiction, *Where the Road Bottoms Out,* and a collection of poems, *Already the World.* She teaches at Sarah Lawrence College and in the M.F.A. program in writing at Vermont College. Victoria Redel lives in New York City with her two sons and the photographer Bill Hayward.

Acknowledgments

I am blessed with many people to thank for their help with this novel but it pleases me most to thank Jonah Redel-Traub for his remarkable insight and continuous, uncanny conversation and Gabriel Redel-Traub who let me borrow his deep knowledge of the magic boy. I thank my agents Charlotte Sheedy and Jonathan Hevenstone for the bounty of their tremendous knowing and efforts. Graywolf Press represents everything I as a writer wanted in a press and I thank their staff especially Fiona McCrae, Anne Czarniecki, Janna Rademacher, and Katie Dublinski for such care, intelligence, and enthusiasm.

Every gratitude to Martine Vermeulen—my dream reader—who read each draft of the novel with a critical and nourishing intelligence. For their generosity and suggestions with the text in various stages, I am grateful to Sheila Kohler, Terese Svoboda, Jill Dunbar, Gordon Lish, Susan Thames, Diane Williams, and Jan Sandler, who proofread the text.

There are not enough thanks I can possibly offer to my remarkable family and friends. You who sustain me, I hope that I honor your gifts with a rigorous bravery and heart.

The text of this book has been set in Trump Mediäval,
designed by Georg Trump and issued in 1954
by the Weber Foundry, Stuttgart.

Book design by Wendy Holdman.
Typeset by Stanton Publication Services, Inc.,
St. Paul, Minnesota.
Manufactured by Friesens on acid-free paper.

The S. Mariella Gable Prize

Graywolf Press is delighted to award the first S. Mariella Gable Prize to Victoria Redel's *Loverboy*. The prize, funded by the Teagle Foundation, is named after a key figure in the College of Saint Benedict's history. Sister Mariella Gable began teaching there in the early 1920s and was a strong believer in the transcendent values of literature. In 1942, she published a provocative anthology, which contained several stories on race relations and an early piece by up-and-coming author, Ernest Hemingway. Gable tirelessly promoted unknown authors—including the emerging work of Betty Wahl and Flannery O'Connor—and was herself a well-respected author and essayist.

The S. Mariella Gable Prize is one facet of the ongoing collaboration between Graywolf Press and the College of Saint Benedict, located in St. Joseph, Minnesota, that began in September 1997. Graywolf Press also plays a prominent role in Saint Benedict's recently launched Literary Arts Institute, which includes author readings and lectures in the Twin Cities and at the Saint Benedict campus, student internships at Graywolf, an author residency program, a Reader's Theater program, and a summer publishing course called Inside Books that runs in July.

Graywolf Press is a not-for-profit, independent press. The books we publish include poetry, literary fiction, essays, and cultural criticism. We are less interested in best-sellers than in talented writers who display a freshness of voice coupled with a distinct vision. We believe these are the very qualities essential to shape a vital and diverse culture.

Thankfully, many of our readers feel the same way. They have shown this through their desire to buy books by Graywolf writers; they have told us this themselves through their e-mail notes and at author events; and they have reinforced their commitment by contributing financial support, in small amounts and in large amounts, and joining the "Friends of Graywolf."

If you enjoyed this book and wish to learn more about Graywolf Press, we invite you to ask your bookseller or librarian about further Graywolf titles; or to contact us for a free catalog; or to visit our award-winning web site that features information about our forthcoming books.

We would also like to invite you to consider joining the hundreds of individuals who are already "Friends of Graywolf" by contributing to our membership program. Individual donations of any size are significant to us: they tell us that you believe that the kind of publishing we do *matters*. Our web site gives you many more details about the benefits you will enjoy as a "Friend of Graywolf"; but if you do not have online access, we urge you to contact us for a copy of our membership brochure.

www.graywolfpress.org

Graywolf Press
2402 University Avenue, Suite 203
Saint Paul, MN 55114
Phone: (651) 641-0077
Fax: (651) 641-0036
E-mail: wolves@graywolfpress.org